"Would You Like Me To Tell Your Fortune, Robert?"

"Do you know how?" Rob inquired innocently, as if he'd never heard that Gypsies were renowned for their ability to see the future.

Serena stood up and walked over to him. Taking his palm in her hands, she traced a line that ran between his thumb and wrist. "In this case, I'm fairly certain I can read what's in store for you without too much trouble."

Her feather-light touch on his palm sent a jolt of sensation up his arm that swiftly aroused him to the point of groaning. He managed to suppress the urge, just barely.

In a heavy Hungarian accent, Serena predicted, "As the snow flies, so will your temper, but there will also be laughter. Some days you will pray for an early spring, but others will make you wish that the snow never melts completely. You will find a friend and an adversary and, if the stars deem it right, your heart's desire."

As he gazed into her eyes, Robert felt as if he were staring into a pair of crystal balls, for his future was clearly written there for him to see. "Then kiss me, Serena," he urged hoarsely. "Kiss me and make my fortune come true."

Dear Reader:

Welcome! You hold in your hand a Silhouette Desire—your ticket to a whole new world of reading pleasure.

A Silhouette Desire is a sensuous, contemporary romance about passions, problems and the ultimate power of love. It is about today's woman—intelligent, successful, giving—but it is also the story of a romance between two people who are strong enough to follow their own individual paths, yet strong enough to compromise, as well.

These books are written by, for and about every woman that you are—wife, mother, sister, lover, daughter, career woman. A Silhouette Desire heroine must face the same challenges, achieve the same successes, in her story as you do in your own life.

The Silhouette reader is not afraid to enjoy herself. She knows when to take things seriously and when to indulge in a fantasy world. With six books a month, Silhouette Desire strives to meet her many moods, but each book is always a compelling love story.

Make a commitment to romance—go wild with Silhouette Desire!

Best,

Isabel Swift
Senior Editor & Editorial Coordinator

JOYCE THIES
Gypsy Moon

Silhouette Desire

Published by Silhouette Books New York

America's Publisher of Contemporary Romance

Books by Joyce Thies

Silhouette Desire

Territorial Rights #147
Spellbound #348
False Pretenses #359
The Primrose Path #378
†*Moon of the Raven* #432
†*Reach for the Moon* #444
†*Gypsy Moon* #456

*written as Melissa Scott
†*Rising Moon series*

SILHOUETTE BOOKS
300 East 42nd St., New York, N.Y. 10017

JOYCE THIES

has authored or co-authored over twenty contemporary and historical novels. Readers might recognize her as the Joyce half of Janet Joyce. She wrote her first Silhouette Desire, *Territorial Rights*, as Melissa Scott, but is now writing under her own name.

While researching a historical about early Montana, Joyce fell in love with the beautiful philosophies held by the Absaroka Indian tribe and wanted to share them with her contemporary readers. While studying the memoirs of Plenty Coups, the last legitimate chieftain of the Absaroka, she was inspired to begin the "Rising Moon" series.

To his biographer, Plenty Coups said, "All my life I have tried to learn as the chickadee learns, by listening so that I might help my people. We love our country because it is beautiful and because we were born here. Remember this, Sign Talker, you have felt my heart and I have felt yours. I want to learn all I can from the white man, for riding with the whirlwind instead of opposing it, we shall save the heartland of our country."

When she read this, Joyce felt the pride and dignity of the Absaroka heart and wished to do as Plenty coups asked Sign Talker, "To write with straight tongue so your people shall come to know mine."

TALES OF THE RISING MOON — BOOK III

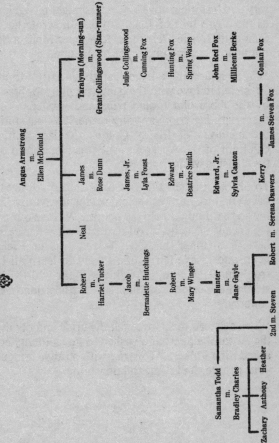

Angus Armstrong
m.
Ellen McDonald

Robert — **Neal** — **James** — **Taralynn (Morning-sun)**
m.   m.   m.
Harriet Tucker   Rose Dunn   Grant Collingswood (Star-runner)

Jacob
m.
Bernadette Hutchings

Robert
m.
Mary Winger

Hunter
m.
Jane Gayle

Robert   m.   Serena Danvers

Samantha Todd
m.
Bradley Charles   Heather

Zachary   Anthony   2nd m. Steven

James, Jr.
m.
Lyla Foust

Edward
m.
Beatrice Smith

Edward, Jr.
m.
Sylvia Canton

Kerry   m.   James Steven Fox

Julie Collingswood
m.
Cunning Fox

Hunting Fox
m.
Spring Waters

John Red Fox
m.
Millicent Berke

Conlan Fox

One

Bluebell was a swaybacked old nag, but the value of the animal wasn't at issue here. Robert Armstrong had involved himself in this perturbing situation as a matter of principle. He was a veterinarian, and he had taken an oath to protect animal health and relieve suffering. That oath applied to all animals, even Harold Rutgers' sorry excuse for a horse.

Unfortunately, Harold believed that some catchpenny gypsy was better able to treat Bluebell's ailments than a trained veterinarian was. At times Robert wished he'd never met Harold, let alone made a bargain with the crotchety old man to board his asthmatic horse in exchange for Harold's services as a gardener. And today was definitely one of those times.

When he'd first heard about his gardener's periodic visits to a self-proclaimed healer who lived in the woods at the far edge of his property, Robert had been amused, but then he'd learned that Harold wasn't the only one who was putting his faith in the useless cures of this female charlatan. Over the past few days, he'd discovered that several other local villagers actually believed that when it came to their beloved pets, the gypsy witch had greater healing powers than Robert could make available to them through his knowledge of modern veterinary medicine. According to the locals, this woman could cure everything from warts to blindness, but, for Robert, her most recent claim had been the last straw. No amount of black magic was going to cure a broken-winded horse.

Robert hadn't had any intention of setting up a veterinary practice when he'd left Montana and moved to this rural section of Connecticut. The goal he'd had in mind when he'd purchased the estate of Laurel Glen from his cousin Kerry Armstrong was to change it back into the successful breeding farm for thoroughbreds that it had been in the past. If his neighbors chose to take their ailing pets to some vagrant crystal gazer, it was really none of his business. But as an ethical member of the veterinary profession, he could no longer stand by and watch this quack take advantage of their ignorance, especially when his own gardener was her chief advocate.

The idea of browbeating an old lady, even one who profited from chicanery, didn't appeal to him very much. But if it came right down to it, she had no right to be on his property in the first place. From what Harold had told him, she intended to stay through the winter, then move on like the transient she was. At the rate she was going, however, she could do a hell of a lot of damage before then. Robert simply wasn't going to tolerate her presence on his land for another day.

As the son of a western cattle rancher, he knew how to handle squatters. He could either do as his older brother Steven had done when he'd come upon a woman living illegally on the Triple A, which was to marry her, or he could evict her. Since Robert couldn't see himself bedding down with some dried up old crone, eviction seemed the far more likely option.

"But you sure could have picked a better time for it," Robert grumbled out loud as he ducked beneath the dripping branches of a swamp maple tree and a few drops of cold water slithered down the back of his neck.

It had been an unusually warm October afternoon when he'd set off for the woods, a humid eighty degrees, but the minute he'd gone a step beyond halfway to his destination, it had started to mist. The mist had swiftly changed to a soggy autumn rain that dumped waterlogged leaves on his head and shoulders while a biting east wind whipped up his hair and slapped his face. The rain intensified whenever he quickened his pace, and he was beginning to wonder if the woman he intended to visit was a close relative of Mother Nature.

He'd yet to explore this portion of his property, and now he knew why. Beneath the giant maple trees, the ground was soft, and it absorbed rainwater like a sponge. It also absorbed his expensive leather loafers and splattered mud on the cuffs of his grey twill slacks. He lost his footing on the slippery leaves and tangled his favorite white sweater so securely in a bramble that, in order to get himself loose, he had to take it off.

Robert tugged and pulled at the material, getting wetter by the minute, and when the sweater finally broke loose, he toppled backward into a thicket of stinging nettles. By then it was raining buckets. The sopping sweater provided some protection from the pelting, so he put it back on before he started running. No, this was definitely not his day.

In the center of the next clearing, Robert spotted a small, slate-roofed cabin and made a dash for the front door. He didn't bother to knock but barged right in, too angry and miserable to care if he scared the daylights out of whoever was inside. As far as he was concerned, the fact that she was going to be dealing with a bad-tempered, soppy likeness of his former easygoing self was her own damned fault.

Robert heard a sharp gasp as he slammed the door shut behind him, but his eyes couldn't adjust fast enough to get a good look at the woman before he pulled his sweater up over his head. His chest and back felt as if they were on fire, and he couldn't combat the urge to scratch his stinging flesh. "If you know so all-fired much about herbal medicine," he ranted, "tell me how to get rid of this infernal itch!"

"What did you get into?" a woman demanded from behind him with a husky, slightly accented voice.

"Stinging nettle," he bit out, staring down at the red rash that was already breaking out on his skin.

Adding insult to injury, the woman laughed. "My grandmother would have told you to smear some goose grease on a brown paper bag and wrap it around your chest, but I'm out of goose grease at the moment. Sorry.''

Robert whirled around to face her, but shock stopped the rude comeback he was about to make. He saw a woman curled up in an easy chair next to the fireplace, but she wasn't the woman he was expecting. If this was the evil-eyed crone he'd come to evict, she was the most comely looking crone he'd ever seen, and her twinkling blue eyes looked anything but evil. Combining those baby blues with soft pink cheeks, an adorable rosebud mouth and a silver-blond halo of hair, she reminded Robert of the littlest angel that he'd once read about in a childhood storybook. Then again, as he noted her interested gaze on his half-naked body, he realized that this feminine cherub was much older and not half as innocent as she looked.

That assessment was confirmed when his eyes left her face to take inventory of the rest of her. The colorful blouse she was wearing was practically indecent, falling off one surprisingly tanned shoulder and showing off a tantalizing amount of satiny cleavage. Her black jeans fit snugly, outlining the sexy curve of her slender hips and showing off a pair of shapely legs. The jeans were tapered above trim ankles, which were each adorned by a thin, gold bracelet.

Suddenly Robert didn't know how he could have compared this woman to an angel. Upon closer study he couldn't find one single thing about her that wasn't sinfully provocative. "Who in the world are *you*?" he managed to ask once he'd regained his equilibrium.

"Serena Danvers," the woman replied pleasantly as she slowly uncurled herself from the easy chair, set down the book she'd been reading and stood up to her far less than respectable height. "And you must be the lord of the manor, Robert the Red."

Taken aback, Rob exclaimed, "Robert the Red? Who the devil calls me that?"

"I do," she said with a cheeky grin. "I named you that after Harold told me how red in the face you became when he mentioned that I was treating Bluebell's asthma."

This is my hornswoggling gypsy? Rob asked himself incredulously, interrupting the end of her statement. "What was that?"

Serena happily repeated herself for him. "Now that I've seen you, I must say the name suits your hair, as well as your temper."

"My hair isn't red, and I *don't* have a bad temper," Robert snapped, getting the distinct impression she considered him vastly amusing.

"If you say so," Serena said, though her eyes twinkled at his tone, and her gaze lingered on his dark auburn hair.

Irritated, Robert was about to launch into a scathing lecture concerning her unprincipled medical ethics, but then his itching skin got the better of him, and he couldn't stand it. Swearing like a mule skinner, he began clawing at his chest and shoulders, twisting and turning his torso in order to reach his back.

"Stop that. Scratching will only make it worse," Serena admonished, marching up to him and taking hold of both his hands. As if he were a petulant boy instead of a grown man who was almost twice her size, she led him over to a round oak table.

"I'm tracking mud all over the floor," he pro-
tested, but she laughed off his concern and disappeared through a door at the back of the kitchen area.
She came back with a towel and tossed it to him.

"You can dry off with that while I see what I can
find to help the itching. I may have just the thing."

Robert accepted the towel, but he wasn't about to
volunteer himself as a human guinea pig for one of her
herbal concoctions. "That's okay," he assured her,
resisting the urge to scratch himself. "It doesn't itch
as badly anymore."

"You're not a very good liar, Robert," she repri-
manded. "Now be good and just sit still for a minute."

Half angry, half bemused by her antics, Robert
watched her climb up on a stepladder, search the shelf
of an oak cupboard and take down a black glass jar.
Warily he eyed the purposeful expression on her face
as she climbed back down, unscrewing the lid.
"What's in there?" he inquired suspiciously.

With a mischievous lift of two delicate eyebrows,
she said, "Trust me, milord. This lowly serf wouldn't
dare harm a single hair on that utterly lovely chest."

Robert didn't know if that disconcerting compliment was meant to catch him off guard, but whether
she'd intended it to or not, it served the purpose.
Openmouthed, he just sat there as she scooped a dol-
lop of white goop out of the jar and began rubbing it
into the skin of his chest. Instantly the itching stopped,
and the raging fever in his flesh began to cool.
"What's in there?" he asked again in a much more
indulgent tone.

Serena cackled like the old witch he'd presumed her
to be. "Not so adverse to my wicked brews now, are
we, milord?" As she posed the question, she bowed
her head as if in deference to the lofty title she'd given
him, though her eyes were sparkling with laughter as
she peered down at him through a veil of thick lashes.

Robert glared at her, insulted by her mockery. "Will
you kindly knock off that lord of the manor stuff.
These aren't the Middle Ages."

Serena's acquiescent nod was ruined by her smirk,
and her next comment revealed her opinion that the
world hadn't changed much for her kind since the
twelfth century. "Gypsies are still considered persona
non grata in most places. Didn't you come here to run
me off your land?" she inquired.

"Maybe," Robert hedged, biting back a sigh of
pleasure as her gentle fingers smoothed over his naked shoulders and her soft palms slid down between
his shoulder blades. "And maybe not."

"Of course you did," Serena countered, and moved
to stand behind him so she could reach the full length
of his back.

The blissful sigh escaped his lips, and Robert gave
himself up to her ministrations. Along with the burning sting from the nettles, her massage was easing the
tension inside him, and his temper was cooling as fast
as his curiosity about her was rising. He was a complete stranger to her, but she revealed no sign of shy-
ness at their proximity, and she touched him with an
easy familiarity that was as relaxing as it was disconcerting.

His skin felt warm and tingly with each smooth stroke of her fingers, and suddenly Robert wasn't nearly so relaxed. Irrationally, illogically, he was surprised by desire, a hot and heavy ache that steadily intensified. Since she was just as much a stranger to him as he was to her, the strength of his arousal was embarrassing, and it made him wonder if the marvelous stuff she was rubbing into his skin contained some sort of an aphrodisiac. Before he made a total fool of himself, he leaned away from her touch.

"Thanks," he said abruptly, and stood up from the chair, making sure he kept his back to her as he searched for his discarded sweater.

"I wouldn't put that back on before it's washed," Serena warned as he picked it up off the floor. "The stinging hairs from the nettle leaves are full of toxin, and you'll just start itching again."

"Oh," Robert said, feeling stupid.

Serena crossed the room and pulled open the top drawer of an old dresser. "You can wear this," she said, tossing him a long-sleeved plaid flannel shirt that was a perfect fit for a man his size.

As he drew his arms through the sleeves, Robert's gaze quickly scanned the rest of the one-room cabin, seeking additional evidence that she wasn't living alone. He wasn't a prude, but, for some reason, the mere thought of her sharing board and bed with another man made him angry. Besides the shirt, he didn't spot any male belongings, but then his gaze landed on the rumpled quilts and sheets in the sagging double bed. Both pillows looked slept on, and he immediately saw red.

"This isn't a shelter for passing vagrants," he snarled. "I own this cabin, and I think it's about time you and yours moved on."

Serena didn't know what had set him off again, but it wasn't as if she hadn't been expecting him to order her off his property. Gypsies were used to this sort of treatment from the *gaje*, but she'd hoped this man would be different. When he'd barged in unannounced, all wet and bedraggled and itching like crazy, she'd still thought him the most beautiful man she'd ever seen. When he'd pulled off his sweater, she'd almost had a heart attack at the sight of all those powerful muscles, glistening with moisture and rippling with the kind of strength developed by years of hard physical labor.

Even though his nose had been decidedly out of joint when he'd first arrived, she could've sworn that besides being handsome, he was normally a kind, understanding person. She never would've had the nerve to tease him like she had if she hadn't noticed the crinkly laugh lines surrounding his gorgeous green eyes and the twin dimples in his cheeks that she'd always assumed were only given to those who were blessed with an effervescent inner joy.

She'd assumed, apparently wrongly, that he shared her love of life and embraced the philosophy of live **and let live. She'd hoped that they would have had a** good time arguing over the proven tenets of science versus the questionable merits of herbal medicine, but she'd been wrong there, too. In his mind she was a thieving beggar, and he couldn't get past the label she carried with her wherever she traveled.

Serena knew now that she'd totally misjudged him, but she didn't feel any anger, only a resigned sadness. All manner of people, even those blessed with the eternal gift of laughter, could be prejudiced. The only sign of her disappointment was the slight slump in her shoulders as she reached under the bed for a large canvas duffel bag.

"You can keep the shirt," she said politely, not looking at him as she pulled out a dresser drawer and started stuffing her clothing into the bag. "It won't pay the rent, but, as you know, we gypsies are notorious for skipping out on our bills. It's probably the only thing of value you'll ever collect from me."

"What in tarnation do you think you're doing?" he demanded.

Serena bit her lip to keep her temper at bay. Boy! When she was wrong about somebody was she ever wrong. "Don't worry. I'm not taking anything that doesn't belong to me," she informed him tartly.

"You're leaving!" he practically shouted. "Now? Just like that? In this downpour?"

Serena glanced over her shoulder at him, her brow furrowed in confusion at his astonishment. "Didn't you just tell me to move on?"

"Well...yes," Robert stammered uncomfortably. "But...I didn't mean right now, this very minute."

Serena shrugged and went back to her packing.. "Now is a better time than later. I'd rather not be out on the road after dark. My Sweet William doesn't have very good night vision, and he hates traveling past sunset."

So there *was* a man, Robert thought, angry with himself for feeling any guilt whatsoever at tossing her out. There were at least two more hours of sunlight, plenty of time for her and her boyfriend to find themselves another love nest. Robert's fists clenched as he was forced to swallow the unpalatable realization that he wanted to know what "William" looked like. "When will he be back?"

"Who?"

"William?"

Robert's curiosity earned him another confused stare. "Back from where?"

Knowing her lover's whereabouts was none of his business, but that he was going to ask anyway only served to increase Robert's temper. "From wherever the bastard goes when he's not here with you."

Serena's jaw dropped, and her brows rose, but when she realized what he'd been thinking, she burst out laughing. "When he's not here with me, my horse is tied up in that lean-to out back."

"William's a horse!"

His incredulity was so great that Serena could only shake her head. She understood that many people thought gypsies were promiscuous, but this man was so anxious to lump her in with the stereotype, he'd leapt to an utterly ridiculous conclusion. This time her teasing words weren't inspired by the faulty assumption that they were kindred spirits. "Technically, since I'm not certain of his origin or the marital status of his parents, I suppose William could be called a bastard, but he's more commonly referred to as a gelding."

Robert couldn't miss the sarcasm in her voice, but it was the pity in her eyes that hit him where it really hurt. "Serena, let me explain, I—"

Serena cut him off with a dismissing wave of her hand. "No explanation is necessary. Everyone knows we gypsies are an immoral lot."

Robert winced at her cutting tone and the look in her eyes. His oldest and closest friend was part Absaroka Indian, and Robert found it difficult to believe that with that experience he could be so insensitive to prejudice. He was overwhelmed by shame at what he'd just said. "I've been behaving like an idiot, but believe me, it had nothing to do with your being a gypsy...well, maybe some of it did...I mean I'm guilty of some preconceived notions, but that wasn't why I wanted to see the last of you."

Not listening, Serena picked up her duffel bag and hoisted it over her shoulder. She passed the kitchen counter on her way to the door and hesitated. She doubted that Bluebell would ever receive her next treatment, but she felt honor bound to give it a try. She owed Harold Rutgers for his kindness toward her, even if the real owner of Laurel Glen had decided to renege on Harold's invitation for her to stay on here until the winter was over.

"Will you see that Harold gets this?" she asked, handing Robert a small box. "Tell him to mix it with Bluebell's feed twice a day."

Robert accepted the box, and she stepped past him as if he no longer existed. Having revealed his prejudice, he was now beneath her notice, and Robert couldn't bear to let her leave thinking so poorly of him—whether he deserved it or not.

"I know how crazy this sounds, and I don't have any right to feel this way, but I was jealous," he burst out desperately as she closed her hand around the doorknob. "That's why I got angry when I thought you were sleeping with someone else."

Serena's hand dropped away from the door, and her duffel bag slipped off her back, hitting her behind the knees on its way to the floor. With an astonished gasp, she plopped down on top of it. "Jealous?" she breathed incredulously, a tiny smile tilting up the corners of her lips. "You were jealous?"

Robert met her startled gaze. "Yes," he admitted reluctantly, just as startled as she was by her unexpected reaction to this news. She was smiling at him like a cat who'd just lapped up a saucer of cream. "That pleases you?" he asked, assuming she would be insulted, only not as insulted as she'd been when she'd thought him a bigot.

"Actually, I think it's quite nice," she told him, propping her elbows on her knees and cupping her chin in her hands. The movement caused her blouse to slip farther down her arm, completely exposing one shoulder.

Rob tried to force his eyes away from that satiny curve, but found that he couldn't.

"What a relief," Serena murmured.

Rob glanced up and saw the blue fire in her eyes as she looked him up and down. The impact of her gaze had him groping for the nearest chair, and he swiftly dropped into it, her heated study affecting him in a way she couldn't possibly miss.

"You're nothing like I expected," Rob grumbled, feeling the heat rising at the back of his neck. He hadn't blushed in years, but his face felt as if it were on fire. His reaction to her was ridiculous. All she had to do was look at him, and he was aroused. "I thought you'd be old and ugly."

Serena giggled, seemingly not offended. "And there we have another one of those preconceived notions."

Rob cleared his throat uncomfortably. "I'm sorry. I don't know what got into me. Usually I don't judge people before I've met them."

Serena gave him a considering look as she stood up. "We're all guilty of that sometimes. I have to admit that I had a far different picture of you before we met."

"How's that?"

She shrugged her bare shoulder. "Oh, I thought you'd be the tweeds-and-wool type, and a bit on the stuffy side. I was told that your family dates way back, and I assumed you'd be something of a snob. Was I ever surprised when you barged in here and ripped your shirt off. Not many New England aristocrats would've done that, no matter how badly they itched."

"The part of my family that dates way back doesn't live here anymore. I was born and raised on a ranch in Montana."

"That explains it," Serena said.

"Explains what?"

"How you look and talk."

Robert waited, and she elaborated. "Every once in a while, I heard a certain twang, and no one from around here uses expressions like 'all-fired' or 'what in tarnation.' And you didn't get that tan or all those muscles being a gentlemen farmer."

Rob squirmed for a more comfortable position in her chair and decided he would be wise to switch the subject away from himself. "Speaking of accents, where did you get yours? I thought gypsies were supposed to sound Hungarian, not as if they just walked out of some upper-crust finishing school."

Serena wrinkled her pert nose at him. "I'm an English gypsy, which is why I don't have exotic brown eyes and black hair."

"I didn't know England had any gypsies."

"*Every* country has gypsies," Serena replied loftily. "My great-grandparents were both English, and so were my grandparents, but my father married an American girl. That's how we got kicked out of the Rom. When my father married a non-gypsy, our entire family became *marime*."

"Would you mind explaining all that?"

"Marriage with a *gaje*, a non-gypsy is considered *marime* or immoral. The Rom believe that the *gaje* are our moral opposites and they lack a proper sense of shame. When my parents got married, all the Danvers became outcasts."

Robert didn't understand completely, but he knew an expression of sympathy was in order. "I'm sorry, that must be hard for your family to accept."

"Not really," Serena denied. "English gypsies were never considered true-blue Rom anyway, and if my family still followed gypsy rule, I wouldn't be allowed to touch a horse."

Robert got the impression that she was deliberately lightening the conversation. "You wouldn't?"

Serena shook her head, trying and failing to look very solemn. "Rom women aren't allowed anywhere near the horses. As soon as a girl goes through puberty, the lower half of her body is considered unclean, and an unclean person could contaminate the animals."

"They actually believe that?"

"To be a Rom, one must follow some very strict rules," she stated gravely, but then her eyes began to twinkle. "I'm quite sure I wouldn't make a very good one."

"Quite," Robert repeated her British intonation of the word. "But you still call yourself a gypsy."

"Only because I make an exceptionally good vagabond."

"And are the rest of your family still vagabonds, too?"

The merry twinkle was instantly replaced by sadness. "I'm afraid I'm the last of the Danvers Drabarnies."

"Drabarnies?"

"That's a female who has a knowledge of medicines."

Robert could sense her grief and didn't probe any further, but Serena answered his unspoken question. "I never knew my grandfather, and my parents died in a car accident when I was eight. My grandmother died this spring, so now I travel alone."

Robert knew that saying he was sorry was woefully inadequate, but he didn't know what else to say. For a second she'd looked so lost and forlorn that he'd wanted to pull her down onto his lap and hold her, absorb some of her pain into himself. But somehow he sensed that she wouldn't appreciate his offer of comfort. He saw her as a bright butterfly, and one couldn't hold a butterfly too tightly without inflicting permanent damage on its fragile wings.

Even as he thought it, he saw that this particular butterfly was poised for flight. "And in this day and age, you still travel on horseback? Don't you own a car?"

Serena laughed. "I drive a wagon, just like the settlers in the days of the Old West. My grandmother was old-fashioned that way. She thought cars were a menace to society, especially after my parents died in a car crash."

Robert thoroughly disliked the picture he had of Serena driving a horse-drawn wagon on the side of some congested freeway at night. He might not be able to stop her from going, but he could try to delay her. At least in the daylight, she and her horse would be easier to see.

"Since William dislikes night travel, why don't you wait until morning," he suggested. "There's no reason to rush."

"You wouldn't mind?" she asked with obvious relief in her voice.

Robert stared into her eyes, sensing an anxiety that had nothing to do with driving a wagon at night, a deep-seated vulnerability that she was desperate to hide. "I've changed my mind, Serena," he told her softly. "If you'd like to stay for the winter like you planned, it's okay with me."

Serena went completely still as he graciously gave in, but then she smiled mysteriously. "Would you like me to tell you your fortune, Robert?"

"Do you know how?" Rob inquired innocently, as if he'd never heard that gypsies were renowned for their ability to see the future.

Serena stood up from the duffel bag and walked over to him. Taking his palm in her hands, she traced a line that ran between his thumb and wrist. "In this case, I'm fairly certain I can read what's in store for you without too much trouble."

Her feather-light touch on his palm sent a jolt of sensation up his arm that swiftly aroused him to the point of groaning. He managed to suppress the urge, but just barely.

In a heavy Hungarian accent, Serena predicted, "As the snow flies, so will your temper, but there will also be laughter. Some days you will pray for an early spring, but others will make you wish that the snow never melts completely. You will find a friend and an adversary, and, if the stars deem it right, your heart's desire."

As he gazed into her eyes, Robert felt as if he were staring into a pair of crystal balls, for his future was clearly written there for him to see. "Then kiss me, Serena," he urged hoarsely. "Kiss me and make my fortune come true."

Two

Serena didn't know what possessed her to behave so seductively, but there was something about this place and the man who owned it that brought out a freedom of spirit in her that she hadn't felt since her grandmother had died. In the long months since then, she'd traveled the same highways and back roads as she had all her life, but the comfort and familiarity she'd once found on them had been replaced by an unease that had constantly dogged her footsteps from place to place. Until she'd arrived here, she admitted. In this old stone cabin in the middle of a secluded wood, she'd finally found some measure of peace and an end to the restlessness that had plagued her.

And something else even more precious. Suddenly Serena knew that this was the man Grannie Heidi had seen in her deathbed vision that last day, the man on whom she could test her female wings without fear, a man she could trust. She should have realized it at once. Robert Armstrong was the one who would teach her what her instincts couldn't provide, but her age decreed must soon happen. Now that she was all alone in the world, she must behave as a mature adult and uphold the responsibilities thrust upon her as the last of the Danvers line.

Serena looked down at the large hand she was holding and brought it to her lips, pressing a soft kiss into the center of his palm. She was almost as astonished by Robert's reaction as he was at having a woman kiss his hand. She felt his fingers jerk convulsively against her cheek, then heard him inhale sharply, and, when she lifted her head, his eyes didn't seem capable of moving away from her face.

And they were such beautiful eyes, Serena thought. As green as the summer leaves, yet more brilliant than precious emeralds. These were the eyes her grandmother had described to her—honest eyes that could look into her soul and see what others could not. She opened her mouth to compliment him on their beauty, but she never got the chance before Robert pulled her down onto his lap and swiftly covered her lips with his own.

His kiss had none of the delicacy of hers, but was warm and hard and fiercely possessive. When he increased the pressure, opening her lips fully to the moist penetrations of his tongue, Serena was shocked, but then he began a soft stroking that overwhelmed her with delight. The gasp of fear died in her throat, consumed by a sigh of pleasure.

She had imagined that kissing a man would be more exciting than kissing a boy, but this was wonderful. This was great. This was fantastic! As always, Grannie Heidi had been right—when she met the right man, she would know it immediately.

Robert felt Serena's arms come up around his neck and her fingers slide into his hair. He felt her slender body move sinuously against him, and it was all he could do not to tumble her down to the floor and make the rest of his heart's desire come true this very moment. He was thirty-three years old and had kissed more women than he could count, but none of those kisses had ever inspired such an insatiable hunger in him. He'd tasted varying flavors of female passion, but never such sweetness as he found in Serena's mouth, and even while he was drinking his fill, he was thirsting for more.

In one part of his mind, a part that had almost stopped functioning when he'd felt her soft lips on his palm, he feared that he was dealing with a woman who was so far out of his league that he would be like putty in her hands, but that hadn't stopped him from pulling her down onto his lap. Serena Danvers was the stuff of his most erotic fantasies, a beautiful woman of laughter and mystery who could satisfy him in ways no other woman would dare. She was a free spirit who did what she wanted to do, and at the moment she wanted him.

As if she were aware of everything about him, she seemed to know all the greatest pleasure points in his body, and each one of her movements, each questing stroke of her fingertips, seemed calculated to incite him beyond control. Eventually, unable to stand the pressure building inside him any longer, Robert raised his head. "Hear that? It's stopped raining," he muttered inanely, struggling to contain the storm still raging in his blood before it consumed them both.

Serena leaned her head languidly on his shoulder and opened her eyes. "Has it?" she asked softly, her expression dreamy as she raised one finger to her mouth and used it to outline her swollen lips.

Robert's eyes followed her provocative motion, saw the tender pink underside of her lower lip glistening with moisture as her finger passed over it, and he stifled a groan. He couldn't tell if she was tormenting him like this on purpose, but he suspected she was, and he didn't want her to know the kind of power she already wielded over him after so short a time. He might want her like crazy, but he refused to be any woman's slave.

"I'd better go," he pronounced gruffly, lifting her off his lap and getting to his feet beside her. Grabbing up his sweater, he headed swiftly for the door, doing his best not to look at the rumpled bed on his way out. "Thanks for the use of this shirt. I'll get it back to you."

Serena wasn't prepared for the abrupt change in his mood or his sudden departure, and she needed to know the cause. "I enjoyed kissing you, Robert," she stated truthfully, her adoring eyes following him like a puppy follows its master. "Are you running out like this because you *didn't* enjoy it?"

Robert stopped dead in his tracks. He was taking the coward's way out, and he knew it, but he couldn't tolerate *her* knowing it. "I'm not running out," he replied evenly. "It's getting late, and my dinner is probably waiting. I don't like to eat cold food, and my housekeeper gets testy when I'm late."

Serena's gasp of surprise sounded natural, but Rob felt that her facial expression was too astonished to be genuine. "You could think about food while we were kissing?"

She knew very well that food had been the last thing on his mind, but Robert refused to give her the verbal satisfaction when he'd already provided her with a humiliating supply of physical evidence. "I skipped lunch today," he stated shortly.

He reached for the door as she appeared to consider that ridiculous assertion, and he was already outside when she reached her conclusion. Unfortunately for his peace of mind, he got to hear it before he closed the door behind him. "Then, next time I'll have to kiss you much better," she said in that husky voice of hers that sent sensual shivers down his spine. "And I will, Robert the Red. I promise you that I will."

Why me? Robert was still ruminating over that question when he reached the stables, and he would have walked right past the building if Harold hadn't called out to him. "Bluebell's coughing again," he announced accusingly, as if Robert were somehow to blame.

Giving up the fight, Robert pulled the small box Serena had given him out of his shirt pocket and threw it at the man. The old nag's condition was chronic, and she was on her last legs, but if Harold wanted to waste his time feeding the animal some useless mixture of herbs, so be it. "Go ahead and mix it with her feed, for all the good it's going to do."

Harold's gray eyes lit up. "Twice a day as usual?"

"Twice a day."

Harold nodded with satisfaction. "Isn't Serena something?"

"She's something all right," Robert grumbled, but his reasons for thinking so had to be far different than Harold's. Since Harold was the one who'd given him the idea that Serena was old, he said, "And far younger than I was led to believe."

Harold's leather-beaten features cracked into a smug smile. "And prettier, too, I expect."

Robert got the distinct impression he'd been set up, and he was about to call Harold on that strong possibility, but then, to his vast annoyance, he noticed that their conversation had drawn a crowd. Bill Murdock, his sixty-year-old head trainer, and three of his exercise boys were standing in the stable doorway, hanging on his every word. "Don't you men have some work to do?"

Mike Reynolds, a freckle-faced kid of nineteen, had the nerve to demand, "You didn't make her leave, did you?"

Robert glared at him as he noticed that Mike was speaking for all four of them. To a man, they were concerned about Serena, and Robert couldn't help wondering how well they knew her. Especially the three who were close enough to her in age that they might have gone to her for something besides her medicinal remedies. "Not today, but that's not saying I won't if she doesn't stop claiming her magic potions can cure anything.''

"The poor girl has to eat," Murdock said, and his stable crew nodded in commiseration with him.

Robert's eyes narrowed. "Are you telling me that you don't actually believe in her mumbo jumbo, but you buy into that nonsense she panders just so you can give her some money?''

"She's no more than a mite," Murdock said.

"And she won't take charity," Mike added.

Robert hadn't heard Huey Stone say more than three words in the year he'd worked for him, but when it came to Serena, the shy young man stood up on a soapbox and made an emotional speech. "Somebody had to do something. She wouldn't even have had any furniture in that place if we three hadn't convinced her that we couldn't afford cash and wanted to make a trade. Billy, here, got her to take that old bedstead so she wouldn't have to sleep on the bare floor, and Mike makes sure she gets firewood twice a week. Otherwise, she'd be chopping her own wood, and she's barely strong enough to lift an axe. I got her that table and a couple of chairs, and next week I'm going to fix that ancient electrical box so she won't be in danger of having a fire.''

"In exchange for what?" Robert inquired as all of his previous suspicions about Serena reared their ugly heads. It was beginning to look highly possible that she was the scheming con artist he'd first thought her to be.

When no one had anything to say, Robert's misgivings intensified. "What do you get for all this?" he repeated, switching his gaze over to Murdock, since that was where everyone else seemed to be looking.

To the man's credit, he didn't back down from Robert's piercing regard. "Serena makes a special mash for the horses."

"*My* horses!"

At his irate exclamation, the group drew closer together, as if they hoped there would be more safety in numbers. Even Harold, who rarely made an attempt to align himself with anyone, joined the club. "Won't hurt 'em. It's done a world of good for my Bluebell," he informed Robert defensively.

All his life Robert had been known as the easy-going one, the coolheaded Armstrong who rarely lost his temper, but those closest to him knew that if he ever did lose it, they'd better look out. These men hadn't known him long enough to understand that the quieter his voice became, the closer he was to throwing an all-out, raging fit. "Murdock, you know how many hours I've spent working up an individualized feeding program for each one of my horses," he said quietly. "And you're telling me that you've taken it upon yourself to feed my valuable animals some unknown variety of mishmash?"

"Most of the vitamins are lost before the feed reaches the mill nowadays," Murdock replied. "I give 'em the mash once a week as a supplement, never that much at a time, and I know what it's made out of."

"Which is?"

"Seaweed and honey."

Since only a day ago Rob had considered buying a commercial brand of feed that contained this same source of vitamins, he wasn't as angry as he could've been. "That's all? You've had it analyzed?"

"I like that little waif, but I also value my job."

Somewhat mollified, Robert said, "Well if you want to keep on working for me, the next time you make a dietary change, or any other kind, as well, you'll consult me about it. Is that clear?"

"Yes, sir," Murdock replied, and his fellow cohorts also nodded their agreement before Robert could voice a similar threat to them.

"Fine." Robert turned on his heel and started walking up the drive toward the house.

"Mr. Armstrong?" Mike called before he'd gotten three steps, and Robert whirled back around, an intimidating expression on his face. "Does this mean we can still use Serena's mash? She counts on that money."

Three pairs of eyes rolled up at the question, and Harold coughed into his hand, but Robert wasn't amused. "Just how long have you already been using it?" he demanded coldly.

Mike found something of great interest to study on the toes of his boots. "About a month."

"Then you might as well keep using it," Robert snapped. He strode swiftly back up the drive, but wasn't far enough out of hearing to miss Harold's mutter. "Don't 'spect this is a good time to tell him how much good Serena's plant food does all his roses."

"Uh-uh," somebody sighed dramatically, and Robert upped his pace. The woman was making money hand over fist! Even though he was dying to know how many other herbal concoctions he was going to discover in use around the place, he wasn't about to ask. It was up to his employees to tell him and risk the consequences.

As he approached the house, Robert's spirits rose as they always did. The gracious, white-stone mansion was nothing like the big rustic log house he'd grown up in, but he'd loved every inch of the place since the moment he'd first moved in. Unused to the stately elegance found in both the exterior and interior, he sometimes felt like a displaced country hick, but that feeling was slowly fading the longer he lived here. His cousin had sold him the furnishings along with the house, and he was still overly cautious when it came to using some of the antique furniture, but he sure liked looking at it. Every chair, table and couch in the place had a story to tell about his Scot ancestors, and Robert spent a lot of time plying Betty Sallinger with questions about their origin.

Before she'd moved to Montana and married their ranch foreman, Conlan Fox, Kerry had hired Betty to be the curator of the museum she'd had built in the old carriage house behind the mansion. Kerry had erected the museum to commemorate the pioneering spirit of the immigrants who'd come over from the old country and eventually carved out a powerful nation from nothing but wilderness. Perhaps because she'd been raised in the East, Kerry had always been more enamored by tales of the wild and woolly cattle ranchers who made up the Western branch of the family than she'd been of the more dignified horse breeders who'd once occupied this house.

For Robert, the exact opposite was true. From the
time he was a boy, he'd dreamed of owning a place just
like this one and raising Thoroughbreds. Now, because Kerry had sold Laurel Glen to him in order to
pursue her own dream, he'd been given the chance to
fulfill his, and there wasn't a day that passed that he
didn't want to thank her for the opportunity. Somewhere down the line, he'd inherited the avocation for
horse breeding, and he would be proud if one day his
portrait hung in the main hall along with all those
other celebrated Armstrong horsemen. Once, these
stables had produced a dynasty of champions, and
Robert was determined that Laurel Glen Farm would
rise to such prominence again.

Robert entered the house through the south portico, hoping he could sneak up to his room and change
clothes before Mrs. Riley caught him. Kerry had left
him with a few legacies that he could have done without, and his sharp-tongued housekeeper was one of
them. Unfortunately, when word had gotten out that
Laurel Glen had a new owner who intended to take up
where the last generation of Armstrongs had left off,
old retainers who'd worked all their lives for the family had come pouring out of the woodwork.

Robert had managed not to rehire most of them, but
his reluctance to employ Harold Rutgers and Eugenia
Riley had fallen on deaf ears. Both had a highly pro-
prietorial attitude about the place, and they'd informed him that they were staying, whether he paid
them a salary or not. He might not like it, but he was
stuck with them.

He almost made it to the staircase leading up the south wing when his ears were assaulted from the rear. "You didn't run her off, did you, Mister Robert?"

This was becoming a very familiar question, and Robert was becoming very tired of answering it. He was beginning to think every person in his employ had heard of his cruel intentions toward Serena and was waiting with bated breath to hear if he'd accomplished the dirty deed. It annoyed him to no end that everyone else seemed to know all about her, when he hadn't even known of her existence until a few days ago. It also enhanced the feeling that he was the victim of a conspiracy of silence.

"No, I didn't run her off," he replied resignedly, then added for the ten thousandth time. "And the name's Rob."

He could hardly believe it when Mrs. Riley's pinched features relaxed and her pursed lips thinned out into a genuine smile. "That's my boy," she commented happily and started back for the kitchen. "I'll broil a big juicy sirloin for you, and have it ready and waiting as soon as you come down from your shower."

In a cheery tone she called back to him over one angular shoulder. "And if you require ketchup, you'll find some in that covered dish to the left of your plate. I absolutely refuse to set that plastic bottle next to our fine Wedgwood. The late Mrs. Armstrong, rest her dear soul, would simply roll over in her grave."

Rob stared after her for a long time, unable to comprehend what he'd just heard. In the space of ten seconds, his hostile status with Mrs. Riley had undergone a radical change. Instead of the keep-your-distance Mister Robert, she'd affectionately called him "my boy," and she was letting him have ketchup to put on the red meat she was cooking for him of her own free will. Normally, when he asked for beef, she went on and on about the dangers of cholesterol.

"My boy!" Rob repeated incredulously. "She actually smiled at me and called me 'my boy.'"

Scowling, Robert mounted the stairs. Somehow Serena Danvers had even managed to melt the ice around his elderly housekeeper's cold heart, something he hadn't managed to do with his best efforts. He'd waited a long time for some sign of friendliness from the woman, but now that he'd finally gotten it, he felt resentful. Obviously he wasn't the only one who'd swallowed Serena's hard luck story, and he was no longer so certain that the protective instincts she inspired in people wasn't part of her normal routine whenever she settled in a new spot.

As he stood under a hot spray in the shower, Robert relived the hour he'd spent with her, and, the longer he thought about it, the more certain he became that he'd been a gullible fool. Serena had played him with an expert's hand, tossing out just enough line for him to hang himself, then reeling him into her seductive net without the slightest trouble. He couldn't help but wonder if his exercise boys had been given a free taste of her sweet mouth in exchange for the favors they'd done her.

Had she told them their fortunes in that seductive voice of hers? Offered the same kind of promises to them as she had to him? "Next time, I'll kiss you better, Robert," he mimicked, enraged when his body responded to the words as it had when he'd first heard them.

Robert turned the water to cold. "Oh, no, little lady, if there is a next time, *I'm* the one who's going to do better, and we're not going to stop with some casual smooching. Like you said, I'm the lord of the manor around here, and I'm the one you'll have to please."

When he entered the dining room twenty minutes later, the pleasant change in his housekeeper's attitude toward him was still in effect. Mrs. Riley was waiting to serve him, which was unusual in itself, since she usually set out his food on one end of the eight-foot long, polished mahogany table, then left the room before he arrived. But even more astounding was her obvious anxiousness to please him. "Medium rare, isn't that right? If I've undercooked it, please tell me," she said conscientiously.

"It looks fine," Robert said, taken aback when the tall, thin-boned woman sat down in the chair to his left and watched him chew his first bite. Under her eagle-eyed stare, he didn't dare talk with his mouth full, so he had to endure several more uncomfortable moments of intense scrutiny before he was able to say, "Would you care to join me, Mrs. Riley?"

"I've already eaten, thank you," she replied, and passed him a huge bowl of mashed potatoes. As soon as he'd served himself, she offered him the thick brown gravy—another of the housekeeper's culinary firsts.

"Eh...then you don't have to stay," he said, flushing when he replaced the silver gravy ladle back in the Wedgwood bowl and splattered several drops of gravy onto the spotless damask tablecloth. "I've got everything I need."

"It does my heart good, cooking for someone who has a decent appetite," Mrs. Riley said, not taking the hint. "Miss Kerry always ate like a bird. I know you like apple pie, too, so I made you one for dessert."

Robert's brows rose at the offer of pie, but even higher upon hearing that he wasn't the only one she referred to with that formal title. Maybe he'd made a mistake in thinking she insisted on calling him Mister Robert because she disapproved of him so much. "This steak is delicious," he complimented, when several more minutes went by without additional conversation. "It's got a smoky taste to it, almost like it was cooked over an open fire. How did you manage that?"

"I marinated it with a special recipe of herbs and spices. Do you really like it?"

Robert had heard the word *herb* far too many times today not to feel wary upon hearing it again. He quickly put a damper on his enthusiasm. "Um...it's okay."

Mrs. Riley sniffed. "From the way you gobbled up that meat, it was far more than okay."

"It was good."

"Better than good," she persisted doggedly.

Robert emitted a long-suffering sigh and wished he'd become a vegetarian before dinner. "Okay, it was great...the best I've ever tasted."

"Serena made up the marinade for me," Mrs. Riley informed him unnecessarily. "She also mixed the seasonings for that marvelous salad dressing you liked so much last night."

"No kidding," Robert said without much enthusiasm. If meat and vegetables were both out, maybe he should try a long period of fasting. He could stand to lose a little weight.

"And she makes those fragrant spice balls I place in your sock drawer."

"Is that so?" Robert had heard that going sockless was a modern trend in male fashion. Wasn't it about time he kept up with the latest styles?

"Your work shirts and jeans wouldn't be nearly as soft or smell as good if I didn't add Serena's all-natural fabric softener to the wash water."

"I don't suppose Laurel Glen would make a good nudist colony," Robert muttered under his breath.

"What was that?" Mrs. Riley demanded.

"I was just wondering where this conversation is heading," Robert said, sensing that she wouldn't appreciate the humor in his last statement.

"Well, after meeting Serena and seeing her deplorable living conditions, I was sure you would see it as your Christian duty to take her in and provide for her during this time of need. The poor child is practically destitute."

If anyone was suffering from need, it was him, Robert thought uncharitably, but the only thing he felt obligated to provide when next he saw that little blond sexpot was a decent bed. "With half the county buying her wares, I think she's doing quite well for herself without my help."

"She'd do much better if she had a reliable income," Mrs. Riley suggested firmly. "She'd be a marvelous help around the house."

"What house?"

Mrs. Riley glared at him as if he were deliberately being obtuse. "This house, of course. We could certainly use the services of a good maid, especially one who can help me with the cooking. When my arthritis is bad, it's very difficult for me to complete my work in the kitchen."

As soon as she'd mentioned the word *maid*, an image had formed in Robert's head of Serena walking into his bedroom, wearing a low-cut white blouse, a skimpy black ruffled skirt and black fishnet stockings. He was shaking his head negatively before Mrs. Riley had finished speaking. "Oh, no, I'm not having that woman living in my house. Not this cowboy. Not on your life!"

Even Mrs. Riley could see that there was no use in arguing with him in the face of so vehement an objection, but her acceptance of his stance brought an immediate return to their previous relationship. "Very well, Mister Robert," she snapped icily. "Breakfast will be served at seven. Please do me the courtesy of being on time."

"Hey! What about that apple pie?" Robert shouted after her.

Seconds later the woman returned with his dessert and slammed it down on the table like a hash slinger at a truck stop. "Certain other people barely have enough to eat," she mumbled under her breath. "And he demands pie. I suppose you want ice cream with that?'' she asked impatiently.

Robert jerked back from the table just in time to miss being scratched as his dinner plate and used silverware were snatched away. "I wouldn't want you to go to any extra trouble, Mrs. Riley," he insisted politely.

The woman peered regally at him down the length of her beetle nose. "I realize that you prefer pie à la mode, but if you want it, you'll have to get it yourself. My fingers are much too painful tonight for me to manage an ice-cream scoop."

"I wonder how much I'd be expected to pay for an assistant ice-cream scooper," Robert grumbled in irritation as he picked up his sterling dessert fork.

"Was there something else, Mister Robert?" the departing housekeeper inquired shortly.

"No, I'm quite content with things as they are, Mrs. Riley. Quite content."

Three

___

Carrying a basket in one hand and a small spade in the other, Serena set off into the woods bright and early in the morning. As a child, Grannie Heidi had taught her that spring was for leaves, summer for flowers and fall for roots. Laurel Glen had turned out to be an ideal place to gather healing herbs, but, unfortunately, before she'd discovered how many varieties of plants grew here, it was already too late in the season for her to collect their leaves and flowers.

As always, Serena loved being outdoors. The turning season had brought beautiful changes to the forest, painting the leaves scarlet and gold, refurbishing the bridle paths with a soft new layer of pine needles. The sugar maples were ablaze, and the morning air felt as if it had been dipped in the cool brook that rambled through the woodland. It was time to say good-bye to the richness of summer.

For Serena, this had been a year of farewells. Saying goodbye to Grannie Heidi had been the most difficult to bear, for the woman had loved and protected her as no other person ever would. After her parents' deaths, her grandmother had been Serena's only family, and, without her, Serena felt adrift, not sure where to go or what to do next. Grannie had always adhered to the old ways even after the Danvers had been cast out of the Rom, and she'd taught Serena to respect them, but that was becoming very hard for her to do.

Without the protection of Grannie's self-inspired reputation as a sorceress, Serena was viewed as fair game for the sexual advances of Rom men who had previously kept their distance, and *gaje* men no longer had to fear incurring the old woman's imposing wrath if they approached her. With Grannie gone, Serena could no longer travel safely to the fairs and carnivals where she'd stopped since childhood. Not long after Grannie's funeral, Serena had learned that even though she wouldn't make them a suitable wife, many men considered her an excellent choice for a mistress.

In addition to that problem, Serena had also discovered that past customers didn't have confidence in her skills as a healer. For forty years they'd dealt with Grannie, not her young apprentice, and few were willing to accept that Serena knew as much about the medicinal properties of plants as her grandmother. In order to survive, she had to sell her herbal remedies, but finding buyers was another story.

Very low on money and frightened by the immediate difference in her status following Grannie's death,
Serena had veered off her accustomed routes. She
traveled to a section of the country where she'd never
been before. While on her way north, she had heard
that the small village of Tewksberry in Connecticut
held an annual flea market, and Serena had decided to
try her luck there. To her delight, people had flocked
to the back of her wagon and purchased her entire inventory of herbal teas, spice balls and sweet-smelling
sachets. She was pleased by her success, but the best
thing that had happened to her that day was meeting
Bluebell and her owner, Harold Rutgers.

Upon hearing the animals telltale wheezing, Serena
had felt obliged to inform Harold that she knew how
to relieve some of Bluebell's distress. Unlike most
people, Harold was open-minded enough to allow her
to feed the horse an unidentifiable herbal mixture.
Bluebell's breathing had immediately eased, and Serena had won herself a fast friend.

She knew now that Harold was the gardener at
Laurel Glen, not the owner as he'd first intimated, but
if not for the old man's kindness, she wouldn't have
gained a small but loyal following of new customers or
found such a fruitful place to spend the winter. The
land surrounding the farm was a mecca for growing
things, a bountiful pharmacy of nature's medicines.
By spring, Serena's inventory of plants and herbs
would be increased tenfold.

Today she had gone in search of herb bennet, which
liked very damp and nitrogenous soil. The roots were
often ground up and added to wine or used in cook-

ing to replace cinnamon and cloves. Serena knew it could also be infused into a liquid that would calm the nerves. After meeting Robert Armstrong, her nerves could certainly use a little calming.

Serena hadn't slept well all week, as over and over again, she'd relived the short time he'd spent in her cabin—or *his* cabin if one wanted to get technical. Legally she supposed Robert was her landlord, but he hadn't mentioned her paying rent when he'd invited her to stay for the winter, and no vagabond worth her salt would volunteer compensation if it wasn't demanded. Besides, she planned to reward him in other ways, ways that would please him far more than money ever could, and, in return, he would help her fulfill the vow she'd made to her dying grandmother.

As she considered the weeks to come, Serena could hardly contain her excitement. She had gazed into Robert Armstrong's green eyes and known that he was the one who would insure that the Danvers line continued. Grannie had promised that, when the right man came along, Serena would just know, and Grannie had been right. From the first moment, Serena had felt the powerful chemistry between them, but Robert's kiss had clinched the matter in her mind. Next year at this time, she wouldn't be alone any longer. A year from now she would be holding the next Danvers Drabarnie in her arms.

Centuries ago in England, the Danvers gypsies hadn't been renowned as healers but as excellent basket weavers. No one could remember the woman who'd been the first herbal healer in the family, but her skills had soon overtaken basket weaving as a

source of profit. From then on, the men in the family
had married women who'd learned the art of herbal
healing from their mothers or grandmothers, and,
when those interrelationships had become too close,
they'd searched farther afield for such women.

The daughter of a famous Gloucester healer, Grannie Heidi had been betrothed to Joseph Danvers at the
age of twelve and married at fourteen. By then the
profits in herbal healing were on the decline, but Joseph had upheld the family tradition, just as his father had before him. After the war, times had been
hard in England, and Joseph had decided to bring his
wife and son Abraham to America, the land of opportunity.

Being English, they were looked down upon by the
Rom gypsies, and Abraham couldn't find a gypsy
woman who would have him. When he'd married an
American girl, the fate of the Danvers family had been
cast. As the daughter of this unacceptable union, Serena wouldn't be considered a fit bride for any Rom,
and since there were so few *gaje* men who could joy-
fully accept the wandering life, she was destined to
remain unwed.

Grannie Heidi had made this clear to Serena soon
after she'd entered her teens, but she'd also stressed to
her that, as the last of the Danvers Drabarnies, it was
Serena's solemn duty to bear a daughter who would
carry on in their time-honored profession. With no
male family members left to guide and protect them,
Grannie Heidi had taken it upon herself to determine
the man who would be worthy of fathering this very
special child. Many had applied for the position, but

Grannie had sent them all packing. Unfortunately, she had died before locating the deserving winner of this honor, and all she could tell Serena about him was that he would be her soul mate, a kind and good man whom she would recognize on sight.

For the first time in months, Serena felt a lightness of heart as she went about her daily routine. She wasn't the least bit concerned that Robert hadn't come back after their first meeting. He might not understand any better than she did, but one day soon they were going to be together. Such was their destiny.

After locating the plant she wanted, digging up its roots and filling her basket, Serena began her walk back to the cabin. This afternoon she would grind the roots down into a fine powder that could be mixed with water. As she stepped out of the trees, she saw Betty Sallinger, and she hurried her pace. After Harold, Serena considered the quiet, bookish woman one of her dearest new friends.

Seeing that Betty had brought her beloved toy poodle along, Serena shouted, "Is something wrong with Putsa?"

Betty shook her head and waited for Serena to come closer before she disclosed the purpose of her visit. "Putsa's fine, and that tonic you gave me has really helped reduce the amount of tearing in her eyes. I told **Robert that, but he refused to listen. He yanked the** bottle right out of my hand and threw it in the trash. I'm afraid he's really on the warpath this time, Serena. He thinks you're no better than a snake-oil salesman who's dispensing fake cures and bilking us all out of our money."

To Betty's surprise, Serena smiled. "Poor Robert, this must be very upsetting for him."

"Poor Robert!" Betty exclaimed. "You won't feel that way about him when he comes down here and kicks you out."

Unconcerned, Serena pushed open the door to the cabin and gestured for Betty to follow her inside. As soon as the agitated woman was seated at the table, Serena put a kettle on the stove to boil. "Don't fret so, Betty," she advised as she placed two cups and saucers down on the table. "You know how it affects your blood pressure."

"I don't know how you can be so calm," the woman complained. "I'm telling you, Serena, if Robert hadn't been called to the stable to oversee the birth of a new foal, he'd be over here right now, ranting and raving."

"I find him quite remarkably handsome when he rants," Serena said as she offered Betty a bran muffin. "And utterly fascinating when he raves."

The older woman remained speechless as Serena poured hot water over the tea leaves in her cup.

As Serena took her seat, she asked, "Why do you look so shocked that I find him attractive?"

Betty swallowed the entire contents of her cup before answering. "He's at least ten years older than you are, Serena, and infinitely more experienced. You should see some of the glamorous women he dates. Please, don't even consider getting involved with him. You'll only get hurt."

"I won't be here long enough for him to hurt me, only long enough to gain something precious," Serena said with a faraway expression in her blue eyes.

If Betty had been worried before, she was even more so now. There was something about this child-woman that brought out all her maternal instincts, which was amazing since she'd never considered herself the motherly type. Even so, within five minutes of meeting Serena, she would have done anything to protect her. "Which is?"

"I can't tell you that, Betty," Serena replied mysteriously. "I'm afraid you'd never understand."

"Try me," Betty pleaded, but Serena was adamant in her silence. "I'm your friend, Serena. Can't you trust me?"

"Not about this," Serena said. Seeing the hurt look on the older woman's face, she added, "And I don't want you to worry about it, Betty. Nothing bad is going to happen to me or to Robert."

"Then you *are* planning to get involved with him!"

"Not in the way you think," Serena said with a secretive smile. "And not if he evicts me."

"If only Harold hadn't started bragging about all the good you'd done Bluebell," Betty lamented. "If Robert hadn't found out about you until it turned cold like it always does here in winter, and we'd already piled up a few inches of snow, he wouldn't even contemplate the idea of eviction. He has much too kind a heart."

"Yes, he does, doesn't he?" Serena retorted happily as she took a sip of her tea. "He's really a very nice man."

Betty reached for the teapot and poured herself a second cup. "Maybe I am better off not knowing what you're up to," she sighed. "But mark my words, Serena Danvers, if you decide to set your cap for Robert Armstrong, you're asking for real trouble."

"I'll remember," Serena said, but she didn't seem the least bit concerned about that possibility.

All week long Robert had tolerated cold food, wrinkled shirts and frigid stares from his housekeeper, but he'd been willing to live with Mrs. Riley's censure. The woman had never liked him much anyway. What he couldn't tolerate was Betty Sallinger's defection to Serena's camp. Of all people, Betty was the last person he'd expected to be suckered into the medicinal claptrap Serena spouted. And Betty hadn't purchased that tonic as an act of charity. Although she was a highly intelligent woman, she actually believed that some bogus elixir was doing her white poodle some good.

"And this time I'm coming prepared," Robert growled as he stalked determinedly across the wide clearing. When he reached the front door of the cabin, he gave a resounding knock and waited impatiently for Serena to answer. Unfortunately, when she did, he wasn't at all prepared for how she would look, and just like the last time they'd met, he could do nothing but stare.

She stood in the door frame, her delicate features lit up in welcome and her hair alight from the glowing rays of the dying sun. She was wearing a pink blouse that clung lovingly to her full breasts, and a colorful skirt cinched in at a waist that was so unbelievably tiny that Robert felt he could span it with his hands. Heaven help him, she was so damned beautiful that she literally stole his breath away.

"You've come about Putsa," she informed him knowingly, grasping both his hands and tugging him inside. "I know that you're skeptical, Robert, and I haven't prescribed anything for Betty's sweet little dog that you wouldn't approve of. You know that white poodles are prone to blindness and that carrots and kelp can be of some help in preserving their eyesight. Since it's a rare dog that will eat those things, I formulated a liquid tonic that can be mixed with their regular food."

"Carrots and kelp," Robert mumbled stupidly as she helped him off with his jacket, tossed it over the back of a kitchen chair, then reclaimed his hand. One small portion of his brain computed the fact that her tonic contained ingredients he might have recommended to a white-poodle owner himself, but the rest of his mind was bogged down in a sensual fog. He allowed her to lead him across the room. When she let go of his hand, he dropped weakly into the lumpy chair behind him.

"Are you still angry with me?" she inquired, lowering herself gracefully onto a sagging red velvet couch, a new addition to the cabin that looked like a discard from some cheap bordello. She leaned forward to wait for his response, providing him with a tantalizing view of satiny cleavage, but when he forced his gaze up to her face, her blue eyes were wide and concerned, as if the last thing she would ever want to do was offend him.

Robert shook his head, obviously confused by the strange effect this woman had on him. Away from her, he was able to think logically—call a spade a spade—but whenever he came face to face with her, he wanted to agree with everything she said. "Betty could go to the grocery and buy carrots and kelp at a much cheaper price," he forced himself to point out. "This supposedly marvelous tonic of yours is nothing but a rip-off."

Serena disagreed. "Pouring a few drops of liquid into Putsa's food is much simpler than cooking carrots and kelp, and then trying to coax the dog to eat them. Betty was willing to pay for the convenience."

Her viewpoint was perfectly credible. What was worse, Robert found that he'd lost his will to fight with her. Sitting here and arguing over the merits of vitamin therapy seemed like a total waste of time. Especially when what he really wanted to do was pull her into his arms and kiss her, find out if her lips were as soft as he remembered, her taste as sweet.

"Paying more for convenience is part of the free enterprise system," he admitted.

Serena clapped her hands together and stood up. "I knew you'd understand once I'd explained," she declared, smiling radiantly. "Betty was so afraid you were going to ask me to leave, but I reminded her that you were a very fair-minded person. You're not the kind of man who'd go back on his promise simply because I'd done something to make him angry. You have far too much integrity."

She was doing it to him again, Robert thought, disarming him with her compliments, deliberately inflating his ego. He didn't recall making her any promises, but if he chose to evict her now, he would feel like a real jerk, which was just as she wanted him to feel. He had to give Serena credit. Few women were capable of manipulating him to the extent she was, and, even though he was aware that she was doing it, he couldn't bring himself to get angry.

However, he *did* want her to know that he wasn't as gullible as she thought. "You left out kind, loyal and trustworthy," he stated dryly.

Serena waltzed away to the kitchen area. "Those, too," she agreed, and if her back hadn't been to him, Robert was sure she would have looked just as innocent as she sounded.

"Yup, I'm a real Boy Scout," he said, wondering what she was up to now.

"Would you care for some wine?" she asked as she turned around and showed him the bottle she was holding in her hand. "I made it myself."

Robert's lip twitched at her impish expression. "Was it a good year for dandelions?" he inquired facetiously.

Serena shrugged. "I don't know, but two years ago was a very good year for grapes, and potatoes if you'd prefer something stronger."

Robert's eyebrows shot up in surprise, then quickly narrowed in suspicion as he considered the ramifications of her last comment. "You also make you own whiskey?"

"My grandmother did, but I'm not as fond of the stuff as she was," Serena replied without hesitation. "She kept a still at our campsite in the Smoky Mountains. We'd stop in there once a year to make a new supply, but I doubt I'll get back that way any time soon. Besides, what's left of the last batch she made will probably last me for years."

Robert raked his fingers through his hair. "Um...didn't anyone ever tell her that running a still is illegal? Or didn't your grandmother consider that a problem?"

"It's not against the law if you only make enough for your own use."

Not up on the statutes pertaining to the distillation of moonshine, Robert couldn't dispute what she said, but he was firmly convinced that some of this home brew had found its way into the elixirs that Serena sold to an unsuspecting public. "Now I understand why Bill Murdock swears by your spring tonic. You're selling white lightning."

Indignant, Serena spoke without thinking. "You might be the man of my dreams, Robert Armstrong, but I *do* wish you didn't have this maddening tendency to jump to such nasty conclusions. I'll have you know that none of my tonics contain a drop of alcohol."

Man of my dreams? Robert rolled his eyes at her blatant attempt to sidetrack him from the issue at hand. "Then you wouldn't mind if I tasted a sample," he said, refusing to succumb to that righteous indignation act of hers again.

If they were ever going to get started down the pathway to romance, Serena realized that she had to get rid of this unwelcome obstruction. Robert's lack of trust angered her. "Very well," she snapped, and decided that romance could wait until he was taught a lesson.

Going to the cupboard, she took down one of several blue bottles and a large glass. She handed both to Robert. "Here you are. Drink your fill," she advised.

Ignoring the sparks of temper shooting from her eyes, Robert unscrewed the cap on the bottle and poured himself a generous amount of clear amber liquid. He couldn't smell anything but a mild spicy odor when he lifted the glass to his nose, but she could've disguised the odor of alcohol with something else. He took a small swallow and was coughing by the time the noxious stuff was halfway down his throat. Seconds later his eyes began to tear, and he was gasping, "Water! For God's sake get me some water."

Serena didn't hurry to help him, but she didn't let him suffer for long. She brought him a tumbler of ice water and watched unsympathetically as he gulped it down. "If you were suffering from a head cold, you'd be feeling much better right now," she informed him. "That cayenne really clears the sinuses, doesn't it?"

"Come here, you little devil," Robert croaked threateningly, still not recovered enough to stand up.

Serena whirled out of his reach, her full skirt flaring up around her legs. "And it causes a very warm feeling in the stomach, which feels good when you've got the chills."

"A very warm feeling," Robert agreed, his skin breaking out in a sweat as he slowly got to his feet. He was hot all right, but he didn't know if it was caused by the peppery liquid he'd just drunk or the glimpse she'd given him of her slender calves and shapely thighs. "And being a generous man, I can't wait to spread some of that heat around."

Serena didn't know if she felt more excited or fearful as he walked toward her, but even if the look on his face made her slightly afraid, she couldn't seem to move. His eyes, the determined way he moved toward her, made her tremble, but she didn't back away. Some things were inevitable.

The distance between them was less than two feet, but as he crossed it, Robert forgot he was angry. In the space of two seconds the imp was gone, and in her place was the sexy temptress, her lips parted in invitation.

"What are you doing to me, Serena?" he murmured, his body responding to the seductive sparkle in her eyes and the sensuous movement of her silvery-blond hair as she tilted back her head in order to look up at him. He was mesmerized by her, totally mesmerized.

"What would you like me to do?" Serena whispered, but she couldn't do anything as he cupped her face between his hands and stroked her smooth cheeks with his thumbs.

Robert bent his head and brushed his lips across hers. "You want me to want you, don't you? You want me to kiss you."

In reply Serena lifted her mouth and touched his lips with a light questing kiss. "You were meant for me, Robert."

If he'd stopped to consider it, Robert might have found something strange about her comment, but at the moment all that mattered was knowing that she wanted him as badly as he wanted her. He lowered his head and kissed her again, and this time he opened his mouth over hers, urging her lips apart.

Serena complied, remembering the first time he'd kissed her, wanting to feel that marvelous pleasure again. Yet, this time the feelings were different, far more intense. As their tongues met and mated, she felt a coiled ache deep inside her, a wondrous longing that increased her certainty that she was doing the right thing. She felt his arms enclosing her as he deepened the kiss, and she not only felt the sweeping fires of passion but the lovely warmth of security. In Robert's strong arms, she felt completely safe.

Robert knew he was nearing the point of losing control when he heard her soft moan and he felt her breasts swelling against his chest. Her hips arched in a slow rhythm with his, and he was on fire for her. Her movements were all seductive woman, yet at the same time, he sensed an innocence in her that made each kiss, each touch of her hands, seem all the more exciting. It was that intriguing mixture of searing passion and sweet innocence that was driving him swiftly over the edge.

"If we don't stop now, we're not going to," he growled thickly, leaving the decision up to her.

She nuzzled against him until she found his mouth. "There's no stopping destiny, Robert," she murmured in that soft husky voice of hers, reminding him that her innocence wasn't real, but a perfected sexual art. He wondered how many other men had been with her, been caught in the fantasy she created, and it became imperative that he make this passing interlude in her life one that she would always remember.

He placed a finger under her chin and turned her face up to his. "Then let my fate be in your hands, Serena, just as yours will be in mine."

Four

Serena's lips trembled as Robert's eyes held hers in an embrace that was as thrilling as the feel of his thumbs tracing her cheekbones and the brush of his knuckles against the side of her neck. The moment she'd been waiting for was upon her, but even though she'd been expecting it, had yearned for this to happen, she wasn't exactly certain what she was supposed to do next. Up until now, things had sailed along quite smoothly, but how did a woman go about asking a man to take her to bed?

As far as she knew, the only way to get what one wanted was to come right out with a straightforward request. "Make love to me," she murmured softly, hoping that once Robert knew she was willing, he would take the lead.

Thankfully he did just that. "Oh, I'm going to," he promised, and lifted her up in his arms. His mouth never left hers as he walked over to the bed. Before he swept aside the patched quilt and laid her down on the sheets, he kissed her with more passionate intensity than ever before. "Tonight you are mine, Serena, *all* mine."

"Yes," Serena whispered, staring up at him with big curious eyes. She watched as he unbuttoned his plaid flannel shirt and drew it over his broad shoulders and down his strong arms. This was the second time she'd seen him naked from the waist up, but this time seemed so different than the last, so much more intimate. Completely enamored by the sight of his magnificent chest, she wouldn't even have noticed that he'd stopped undressing if he hadn't said something.

"I assume you're protected."

Serena's eyes darted to where his hand was poised over the buckle of his jeans, and she realized that if she responded negatively, Robert would leave her. She didn't want to lie to him, but she couldn't let him go, not now when she was this close to fulfilling her vow. "Don't worry," she assured him, and he took that evasive answer as a yes.

After that, Serena was only given a few seconds to marvel over the rest of his naked beauty, before he lay down beside her and began swiftly undoing the buttons of her silk blouse. He slipped it from her shoulders and immediately dropped his head to press kisses into the hollow of her throat, making her gasp in delight. Every touch of his mouth or fingers pleased her in ways she never could've imagined and reduced her fears at the same time.

I'm doing the right thing, she repeated to herself over and over again until the wonderful sensations coursing through her body overcame all lingering doubt.

"You're so lovely," Robert whispered, compounding pleasure with pleasure, as his head bent lower toward one of the pink crests crowning her breasts and his fingers teased the other. "So very..." His voice trailed off as he enveloped her nipple with his mouth.

Serena moaned softly and closed her eyes, burying her fingers in the crisp thickness of his dark hair. He was drawing strongly on her, his tongue teasing even while he suckled with erotic fierceness. She was vaguely conscious of his hand at the back of her skirt, but she couldn't help him remove it. The rapturous feelings he was creating with his mouth were so overwhelming that she couldn't move.

He nibbled at her, arousing new and unexpected twinges of pleasure, and she lifted her hands to his back, clutching him desperately. It was as if there were some kind of powerful connection between her breasts and the very core of her womanhood, for with each tiny bite, each swirl of his tongue against her sensitive nipples, she experienced an urgent ache at the juncture of her thighs. She had read enough books to know that making love could be wonderful, but nothing in her imagination had prepared her for this kind of excitement.

Lost in the responses of her own body, Serena didn't realize she was completely naked until she felt one of

Robert's large hands cupping her buttocks, squeezing and releasing as he buried his lips in the curve of her throat. With his other hand, he touched her in ways she'd never dreamed a man would touch her, and unbelievably she felt no embarrassment when his fingers gently stroked her most delicate flesh. It felt too good to be bad.

Serena trembled at the newness of what he was doing to her, but the real shock came when she felt his manhood, hot and heavy against her thigh. She had done very little to please him, and yet he seemed to be just as excited as she was. She could feel it in his rapid breathing, in the searing heat of his skin against hers, and he confirmed it with his husky whisper.

"I'm not going to last much longer," he rasped. "Not this time."

"Oh, Robert," Serena sighed, deciding that sex was unfair for the man, since she had done next to nothing to arouse him while he'd done so much to pleasure her. Somehow, it just didn't seem right that such a lovely experience should be so one-sided.

Robert had no idea that she was concerned about pleasing him when he was so anxious about not pleasing her, and he took her sigh as one of disappointment. Not wanting to suffer by comparison to her previous lovers, he had been ruthlessly determined to bring Serena to climax before he took his own pleasure, yet he was very close to losing control. He didn't know what it was about this woman, but he lost his head whenever he came near her, wanting her as he'd never wanted a woman before.

After only a few moments of feeling her satiny skin against his, his body had been conscious of only one purpose, one tension, and it had to be relieved or he would explode. "Next time," he promised her hoarsely. "Next time will be for you."

As he parted her thighs and positioned himself between them, the tension escalated into an almost brutal fierceness that drove him on a frenzied search for completion. With a low groan, he drove forward . . . and through! In shock, he realized her *actual* innocence, but by then it was too late to stop, and he lost himself in a frenzy of passion more intense than any he'd ever experienced in his life.

Serena was awed as she watched his face, then even more awed as the discomfort passed and the pleasure returned. With each of his powerful thrusts, she was carried higher and higher, and then so high that she cried out in wonder. The world was spinning away from her, and she had no choice but to close her eyes and surrender herself to the swirling glory of sensations that exploded inside her.

It took her a long time to recover, but Robert seemed to be having the same difficulty, so Serena assumed that the lethargy she felt was natural. His breathing was labored, and his body was draped so heavily over hers that she couldn't move even if she'd wanted to, which she didn't. More than the unbelievable pleasure they'd just shared, she loved the feel of his warm skin against hers, the marvelous security of being held in his strong arms and the intimate connection that made her feel so much a part of him.

Eventually Robert managed to lift his head and look down into Serena's face, scowling when he noted the tears brimming in her big eyes. "For God's sake, why didn't you tell me?" he asked, but the question sounded more like an accusation, and his next words confirmed his anger. "Damn it, Serena! Why?"

Serena hadn't thought about the aftermath of their lovemaking or considered the possibility that he would ask difficult questions and demand answers. Her grandmother had told her that men were only after one thing and didn't care how or why they got it, just as long as they did. She should have known that Robert wasn't like that. He *did* care, and he wasn't going to be satisfied with any explanation but the true one. Something told her that he wasn't going to be very pleased when he heard it.

In an attempt to buy herself some more time, she mumbled vaguely, "I . . . I'm not exactly sure."

"The hell you aren't," Robert raged, then lifted himself off her. A second later he was sitting up on the mattress and pulling her up to face him. "This is what you had in mind from the first moment I walked through that door, and we both know it. You deliberately led me on, made me believe that you were an experienced woman, because you wanted this to happen."

Seeing her lower lip tremble, Robert suspected something that made him feel as if he'd just been punched in the stomach. "Exactly how old are you?" he demanded.

Serena lowered her head. "Old enough."

"How old?" he persisted.

"Twenty-three."

"Good lord." Robert winced as his suspicion was confirmed. How could he have been so blind not to sense the naïveté beneath her seductive behavior? Even though he was more angry with himself than with her, he still grabbed hold of her shoulders firmly. "Why on earth would you allow me to hurt you like this, Serena?"

Serena's eyes went very wide. "Hurt me? You didn't hurt me, Robert. I loved everything you did to me." She could tell he didn't believe her, so, blushing furiously, she elaborated, "Especially when you were insi...I...um...especially liked the last part."

Robert still intended to get to the bottom of this perplexing situation, but he was so relieved to hear that he hadn't hurt her that he let himself be sidetracked from the main issue. Wearing nothing but a pink blush, this woman was the most enticing thing he'd ever seen, and he couldn't resist the urge to reach up and tenderly brush her damp cheek with the back of his hand. "If you liked the last part so much, why the tears?"

"Because it was so beautiful," Serena replied honestly, totally unconscious of her nakedness as she came up on her knees and clasped her hands together in front of her breasts. "Will it feel like that the next time?"

"Next time?" Robert groaned incredulously, unable to look at her without wanting her all over again. Then he saw where her eyes were centered, and he realized that she was fully aware of his renewed desire.

Exasperated, he jerked the sheets up over his legs. "There's not going to be any next time!"

"Why not?" Serena asked indignantly. "You enjoyed it as much as I did, and you'd like to do it again."

"Of course I enjoyed it," Robert snarled, holding on to his anger like a protective shield, hoping it might save him from responding to that come-hither look in her eyes. "Any man would take what you just offered, but this one happens to have a conscience. Making love to a woman who knows the score is one thing, but I'm not in the habit of seducing innocents."

Serena turned up her nose dismissively. "It was I who seduced you, Robert Armstrong. As far as my innocence is concerned, let me remind you that I'm not a virgin any longer, by my own choice."

Robert squeezed his eyes shut and lifted his hand to massage away the sudden pain in his forehead. "Why me?" he beseeched the heavens, but, when it came to his dealings with this provoking female, the Fates still had no answer for him.

By some stroke of good luck, Serena didn't realize he was posing a rhetorical question. "You wouldn't believe me even if I told you."

Robert's eyes shot open. "Try me," he suggested in a tone that brooked no argument.

"You're not going to like it," she predicted nervously, realizing for the first time that following one's destiny could present a whole series of unforeseen complications.

"I don't like it now," Robert told her, his expression so threatening that Serena scooted backward out of his reach.

Robert let her go, but as soon as her shoulders were pressed up against the headboard, he moved into position beside her, wedging her between him and the wall. That done, he pulled the sheet up over them both. "Okay. Let's hear it."

Hearing the suppressed violence in his voice, Serena hoped she was already pregnant, because once she explained things, she didn't think Robert was going to make love to her ever again. "Well, considering who I am, it's not likely that I'll ever get married," Serena began, but Robert interrupted her before she could explain.

"What do you mean 'considering who you are'?"

Impatiently Serena told him why she wouldn't make an acceptable bride for a gypsy and why she wouldn't be able to find a suitable husband among the *gaje*. "I'm afraid that the spirit of freedom passed down to me runs very deep, and I'll always be a wanderer," she concluded firmly. "What sort of man would be willing to give up his home and take to the roads for the rest of his life?"

"A man who likes to travel."

"And one who wouldn't mind living out of my caravan trailer for nine months of every year?"

Robert considered that stipulation and conceded, "Okay, if those are your qualifications, the field is probably pretty narrow."

"The field is barren, Robert," Serena corrected. "My grandmother spent the last five years of her life searching for the right man for me, but she never found him.''

Wisely, Serena didn't add, *until she saw you*. Robert looked confused enough as it was, and she didn't want to make matters worse. The part about Grannie's vision could wait until she'd laid down some additional groundwork. If she could just make him understand how important a child would be to her, perhaps he wouldn't be as angry as he'd been when he'd discovered she was a virgin. After all, he was a member of a proud family himself and should be able to empathize with the duty she felt toward hers.

"We traveled all over the country in search of a husband, but Grannie rejected every man who showed an interest in me. None of them were right," she concluded emphatically, showing no sign of resentment that this decision had been made for her by someone else.

"Didn't you have any say in the matter?"

Serena shook her head. "Normally it's a girl's father or some other male family member who chooses her husband, but, as I told you, Grannie and I were the last of the Danvers, so that responsibility fell to her."

Robert exclaimed, "And you accepted that without question?"

"Of course," Serena said. "My grandmother loved me. She never would have chosen someone that I couldn't be happy with."

Robert shook his head in disbelief. "This sounds like something right out of the Dark Ages! You mean to tell me that gypsies still arrange marriages for their daughters?''

Serena tilted up her nose in disdain of his incredulity. ''These matches usually work out much better than your *gaje* marriages. Gypsies don't have a fifty percent divorce rate. When we marry, the bond lasts forever.''

All this talk on the subject of marriage and long-lasting bonds was making Robert extremely nervous. ''So now that your grandmother is gone, are you still looking for the right man to marry?''

''Not to marry. I've given up on that possibility,'' Serena replied, missing the look of relief that passed over Robert's face.

Certain he was now on the right track, Robert said, ''So you're not planning to marry, but you didn't want to live your whole life without knowing what it was like to make love, and I was chosen to be your teacher?''

Serena took a deep breath. If she let him go on believing that all she wanted from him was some sexual tutelage, there was a far better chance of her being on the receiving end of future lessons, but lying had never come easy for her. As it was, she was already guilty of evading the truth after he'd asked her about birth control, and she knew that she wouldn't be able to live with herself if she attempted an even greater deception. ''I *did* want to know what it was like, but there's something else I wanted much more.''

Robert's eyes narrowed. ''Which is?''

Before she lost her courage, Serena said, ''I might not be able to find a husband, but that doesn't mean

I can't have a child. As the last of the Danvers, it's up to me to make sure my family doesn't die out.''

Robert's expression remained blank for several seconds. Then her words sank in, and the blood rushed to his face. "Stud service!" he shouted. "You came to me for stud service!"

"You make it sound so crude, but it's not like that at all," Serena came back defensively. "Our being together was meant to be. The day she died, Grannie had a vision, and she saw the father of my child."

"Me!"

Serena nodded. "As soon as I met you, I knew you were the man she'd described to me."

It took a tremendous effort, but Robert managed to stay calm. In a deadly quiet tone, he reiterated what he'd just heard. "Let me see if I've got this straight. While on her deathbed, your grandmother gazed into her crystal ball, and, out of all the men in the world, she saw me?"

Serena glared up at his mocking face. "I told you that you wouldn't believe me."

"You've got that right," Robert grated. "That's the most ridiculous story I've ever heard."

"Grannie Heidi had the second sight," Serena informed him haughtily. "She told me all about you."

Robert tried to remember if he'd run into some dotty old lady within the past year or so, but if he had, he couldn't recall it. It was far more likely that Serena's grandmother had filled her head with some romantic notions about a tall, dark and handsome stranger who would soon enter her life, because she'd been worried that after she was gone, Serena would be alone and terrified. It was also Robert's guess that the old woman had felt guilty for keeping Serena all to herself for so many years and for selfishly turning away every man who'd shown the slightest interest in her. In a belated attempt to offer Serena some hope for the future, the woman had concocted this vision baloney. "Tell me exactly what she supposedly saw."

"Grannie said you'd be very handsome and have beautiful eyes that could see beyond my face to what's in my heart. She also said that we'd be soul mates," she said reverently.

"Oh, Serena," Robert sighed, deeply moved by her naive belief that he was the man in her grandmother's vision. He didn't have the heart to tell her that her beloved Grannie had fed her a line of generalities that might be applied to almost anyone. "Is that how you really see me?" he inquired gently. "As your soul mate?"

"I wasn't completely positive before we made love, but I certainly am now," she affirmed. "Grannie was absolutely right about everything. She said that I'd know when I'd found the right man by the way he'd make me feel, and you made me feel so wonderful, Robert, so beautifully free. It was almost like flying. I know you're the man she saw."

"You do," Robert said, and it wasn't a question. There was no doubt in his mind that she believed everything that she was saying.

"You're the man who will give me my child."

As he listened to the conviction in her voice, the dull pain in Robert's head sharply intensified. "I suppose your grandmother saw this baby in her vision, too?"

"A beautiful baby girl and the next Danvers Drabarnie," Serena proclaimed with absolute certainty.

Robert didn't know what to say to these crackpot notions of hers. Of course, he was glad that she'd enjoyed their lovemaking and relieved that he hadn't ruined her first time, but the assumptions she'd drawn about him and this baby girl they were supposed to have created were downright crazy. He wasn't this mythical dream man she'd been searching for, and no way in hell was he going to father her child.

For one thing, Serena was still too much a child herself to handle the challenges of motherhood, but there was something besides her incredible naïveté that made it difficult for Robert to see her as a parent. He felt as if he were dealing with a woman who'd just dropped into his life from a past century, and he didn't have a clue how to deal with her. At the same time as he reached that frustrating conclusion, he was struck by another very disturbing thought.

Grabbing hold of her wrist, he demanded, "You lied to me about using birth control, didn't you?"

"It wasn't exactly a lie," Serena replied with a startled gulp. "I said you didn't have to worry, and you don't. I plan to be solely responsible for my daughter."

"*Our* daughter!" Robert exploded without thinking. "If I've made you pregnant, the child will be just as much mine as yours, and I'll be equally responsible."

"That's very kind of you, Robert, but you don't need to feel any sense of obligation. Once I leave here, you won't even know where we are," Serena pointed out, hoping her reasonable tone would have a calming effect on Robert. "If you like, I can promise that I'll never come back this way again. You can forget you ever met me."

Robert stared at her. She thought she was making him a generous offer! It took a deliberate effort, but he managed to control his temper and not throw such an outrageous overture back in her face. He forced himself to remember that Serena had been raised under an entirely different moral code than his own, and getting angry about it wouldn't serve any purpose. Even so, he couldn't let her go on believing that a situation like this could be worked out so simply.

Letting go of her arm, he stated quietly, "Any child of mine will stay with me, Serena."

Serena shook her head. "But that wouldn't be possible."

"Exactly," Robert replied. "And that's why, no matter what your grandmother saw to the contrary, the two of us weren't meant to conceive a baby. I'm sorry, Serena, but I could never allow you to bear my child, then watch you take her away from me. I have some very strong convictions when it comes to family myself, and one of them is that my children will grow up under my roof."

Robert meant what he said, Serena knew, and she felt a sick dread. "And if I'm already pregnant?"

"Odds are you aren't."

"But if I am, you'd fight me for the baby?"

"I'd not only fight you, but I'd win," Robert stated arrogantly.

Of course he would, Serena acknowledged in silent misery. With Robert's money and position in the *gaje* world, if it came down to a battle for custody, she wouldn't stand a chance. For the first time, she questioned her grandmother's happy predictions for her future, and with her doubt came a crashing disillusionment. What if Grannie had made the whole thing up? What if she'd never had a vision at all?

Robert watched as a while series of emotions passed over Serena's face, washing away all the color and leaving her big blue eyes looking wounded. He felt as if he'd just kicked a helpless kitten who couldn't understand such an act of cruelty. But then, the second before he would have pulled her into his arms to offer what comfort he could, he saw the frantic movement of her eyes, and he realized what she was planning.

Rolling off the bed, Robert picked his clothes up off the floor and quickly got dressed. He hated what he was about to do, but he had no other choice. "Don't even think about leaving here, Serena," he commanded. "Like it or not, until I know for sure that you're not pregnant, you're going to stay put."

All her life, Serena had been free to come and go as she chose. Having that freedom taken away even for a short time filled her with an odd sense of panic. "It's a free country," she felt compelled to say, even knowing that her small show of defiance wouldn't make any difference to Robert or change her current situation. She had seen the ruthless expression in his eyes when he'd realized that she was intending to flee as soon as he left the cabin. No matter how she felt about it, she was going to be his prisoner until such time as he decided to let her go.

"If you take off, I'll find you and haul you right back," he promised, just as Serena knew he would. "Why don't you save us both the aggravation."

For a moment their eyes met and held, conveying the emotional tumult they were each feeling. As he gazed into her soulful blue eyes, Robert felt worse every second, and he was the first to break the contact. "You were planning on staying for the whole winter anyway," he reminded her. "So nothing's really changed."

"Everything's changed," Serena replied softly.

With his jaw clenched, Robert walked over to the chair where Serena had hung his jacket and put it on. "Welcome to the real world, Serena. You were bound to run into it one day. I'm just sorry I was the one who had to shatter the dream world you've been living in."

"Me, too," Serena whispered, reaching for the quilt as a chill swept up her spine.

Noting the tremble in her lower lip, Robert wanted to stay, almost as much as he wanted to leave. She looked so damned young and so hurt, but it was beyond his means to change either of those conditions. "Sooner or later, everyone has to learn that you can't have the freedom without accepting the responsibility. Paying the price for our actions is part of growing up."

Serena didn't know how much longer she could hold on to the tears that were threatening, so she nodded her head in agreement in the hopes that he would leave before she broke down.

Robert saw how close she was to tears, but he also saw the valiant effort she was making to restrain from crying. "I'll come by tomorrow," he said for lack of anything better to say, but Serena gave the words a far more sinister meaning than he'd intended.

"That won't be necessary," she told him. "I'll save us both the aggravation and give you my solemn word that I won't try to leave until I'm sure it's okay to go."

Robert sighed heavily. "I'll come by tomorrow," he repeated. "Not because I don't accept your word, but because I want to make sure you're all right."

"I'll be fine," Serena insisted proudly, and Robert left without even bothering to acknowledge such a dishonest claim.

Five

On principle, Serena should have left Laurel Glen the minute she discovered that she wasn't pregnant, but instead she'd found herself making one excuse after another to delay her departure. It had been over a month since she and Robert had made love, but her reasons for staying on had nothing to do with him. The call of the road just wasn't as strong when the weather turned cold. In the wintertime, even the wildest of creatures stayed in their warm dens. At least, that was what she'd told herself.

It had first been the huge snowstorm that had arrived on the day after Thanksgiving that had prevented her from leaving. Then she'd accepted an invitation to Mrs. Riley's seventieth birthday party on the fifth of December. After all, the irascible woman had so few people who'd been willing to share that exalted occasion with her. A week later Betty had fallen ill with the flu, and, since her friend didn't have any family near-by, Serena had felt obliged to sit with her until she'd gotten back on her feet.

Since then, several other complications had cropped up that had required her medicinal skills, including Bluebell's latest asthma attack and Bill Murdock's laryngitis. She realized those minor problems wouldn't have prevented her from leaving if she'd truly wanted to go. Much to her surprise, being stuck in one place hadn't turned out to be half as bad as she'd thought it would be. In fact, she'd found out that she enjoyed being surrounded by so many people, good people, who not only needed her but cared about her as if she were a close relative. If she left Laurel Glen before Christmas, all those caring people would be hurt.

All but one, Serena amended, as she considered her most recent encounter with Robert. At the moment she was sure that he would be happy to see the last of her, but he would come around eventually. Once he got over being angry with himself, she was confident that he would realize what she'd accepted already. No matter how Robert fought against his feelings, it wasn't over between them.

For a day or so after they'd made love, Serena had been too upset to notice the distinct change in Robert's attitude toward her, but once she'd calmed down, it hadn't taken her long to realize that he no longer viewed her as a mature, desirable woman, but as a young, sexless child who needed looking after. At first she'd tried not to let it bother her, but her resentment had grown with each day that had passed. Just as he'd promised, Robert had come by to see her the next day and every following day, not just to check up on her whereabouts, but to get the cabin into better condition than any place she'd ever stayed.

Of course, she was grateful for the electric heater that kept the cabin warm even when there wasn't a fire burning in the fireplace, and for the new hot-water heater that insured her faucets could always be counted on for hot water. Any person would appreciate having a roof that didn't leak when the snow melted, lights that didn't flicker and a toilet that stopped running after it was flushed. What Serena didn't like was being treated like a helpless, dim-witted waif, and yesterday had been the final straw as far as she was concerned.

It was only out of politeness that, before then, Serena hadn't told Robert she was as capable as he was of changing the washers in the sink, weatherproofing the door and repairing broken furniture. Since she'd been doing such tasks for most of her life, she was probably even more capable at some things, which had certainly been proven yesterday. In his guise as a concerned landlord, Robert had arrived with a roll of plastic to cover the windows and had discovered her lying on her back, with her head and arms thrust inside the counter below the kitchen sink.

She'd been unaware of his presence until he'd grasped hold of her ankles and pulled her out. "What the hell do you think you're doing?"

"The pipe is clogged," she'd informed him, but before she could elaborate on the problem, he'd snatched the pipe wrench out of her hand and had taken over the job himself.

Angered by his high-handedness, Serena hadn't told him that she'd yet to turn off the main valve. With one twist of the wrench, Robert had gotten himself a snootful of water. While he'd flailed around trying to escape the cold spray, she'd calmly reached under the counter and shut off the valve. Even then he hadn't seen fit to admit his incompetence as a plumber, but had gone right back to work, unscrewing the joints and earning himself another dowsing, this time with nothing so pleasant as water.

Prepared for just such an occurrence, Serena had presented him with a towel. Then, while he'd made a vain attempt to wipe the grime off his face and chest, she'd completed the job he'd messed up. Even a man half-blinded by sludge could tell that she was proficient in the task, and Robert was a big enough man to acknowledge a job well done. Unfortunately, instead of basking in his compliment, she'd taken one look at his greasy hair and the black globs all over his shirt and had burst out laughing.

It was then that she'd changed back into a woman in his eyes. At the sound of her husky laughter, Robert had lost his temper and also the strict control he'd apparently been keeping on his behavior around her. Before she'd realized what was happening, her giggles had been smothered beneath an angry male mouth. Moments later, when it had become obvious to them both that a single kiss wouldn't be enough to satisfy either of them, Robert had sworn viciously under his breath, thrust her away from him and stalked angrily out of the cabin.

Smiling at the memory, Serena wondered how long it would be before she saw him again. According to the insatiable hunger she'd felt in his kiss, she didn't think he would hold out very long, which was just fine with her. That kiss had shown her that Robert wasn't the only one who'd been hiding his feelings.

Even knowing that he wasn't going to give her a baby, Serena still wanted to make love with him again. During the day, she'd managed to suppress that longing, but at night it was all she ever dreamed about. Now she had reason to believe that Robert shared those dreams. If he still desired her as much as she desired him, it was just a matter of time before her dreams turned into reality.

In far less time than she'd expected, her front door burst open to disclose the first rays of morning sunlight and a very disgruntled-looking lord of the manor. Robert burst out without preamble. "You're ten years younger than I am!"

Sitting up straighter on the velvet love seat, Serena shrugged her shoulders, and the crocheted comforter she'd wrapped around herself fell off, revealing a white flannel nightgown that made her look even younger than she actually was. "I'm over legal age."

Robert groaned, "Compared to me, you're a babe in the woods."

"As you said, everyone has to grow up sometime."

"Don't you have any sense of self-preservation?" he demanded, raking one hand through his hair in frustration.

"It's you who's taking a chance," Serena stated softly. "I'm here today, but I may be gone tomorrow."

Robert closed his eyes. "We come from completely different worlds."

"Opposites attract."

"I don't have meaningless affairs," Robert bit out.

"Neither do I," Serena retorted.

For a moment there was absolute silence between them, but then Robert released his breath in a little explosion of tension. "Dammit, I told myself I wouldn't do this," he growled as he stepped completely over the threshold and closed the door behind him. "But I can't keep up this pretense any longer."

"I'd be extremely grateful if you didn't," Serena told him saucily, her admiring gaze telling him that, even in a rumpled work shirt and jeans, his face covered by a night's growth of beard, she still liked what she saw.

"I want you, too," he confessed, looking none too pleased by the admittance. "I can't sleep nights for wanting you."

"If you'd really rather not have me, I could make up a soothing draught that might help you rest," Serena offered magnanimously, and, for the first time, Robert grinned.

"Lately I've consumed enough alcohol before bedtime to fell a bull moose, but all I ever achieve from the effort is a bad hangover the next morning."

Serena smiled back. "Mrs. Riley told me that you'd developed a sudden fondness for the evil brew. She's been very worried about you."

That produced a wholehearted laugh. "If that woman is worried about anything, it's that I might get sick all over the Persian rug next to my bed. As far as she's concerned, my plebeian feet are unworthy to touch it."

"She *does* seem to be awfully attached to furnishings," Serena agreed. "But maybe that's only a front to hide the fact that she gets even more attached to the people who own them. She really thinks the world of you, Robert. Without her job at Laurel Glen, she would have no place to go and nothing worthwhile to do. When you agreed to hire her, you gave her back her dignity."

Robert was incredulous. "She actually likes me?"

"She adores you," Serena amended, glad to tell him what everyone else already knew. "Maybe even more so than Harold, who can't say enough about you. After listening to him go on and on about your sterling character, I expected to see you walking on water the day we met."

"Amazing," Robert observed, but even though he was glad to hear how his two most cantankerous employees actually felt about him, he was anxious to learn how Serena felt. Crossing the room, he sat down beside her on the love seat. "But, as you promptly found out, I'm no saint."

Serena saw the question in his eyes and knew what he was asking. "And you found out that I'm no angel. I'd say that makes us even."

"You're sure?" Robert asked, staring into her eyes.

"I'm not a child," she reminded him, just in case he was still clinging to that ridiculous conception. "I want to make love with you again. What we shared the first time was so incredibly beautiful, it couldn't be wrong. Even if we're together for only a short time, it will be a time I will always cherish.''

Robert knew he would, too, but before he gave in to his raging desire for her, he had to make certain of one more thing. "If your grandmother *did* have a vision, Serena, I'm not the man she saw."

Serena sighed, but there was no sadness in the sound. "My grandmother loved me. I understand now why she made up such a thing," she said without bitterness. "Since I was eight, it had been just the two of us, and we were very attached to one another. She knew how I would grieve for her, and she wanted to provide me with faith in the future. She wanted me to look forward, not dwell in the past."

The interpretation Serena had put on her grandmother's behavior was much kinder than the one he would've put on it, but if that's what Serena wanted to believe, Robert was willing to accept her version. At least she was no longer deluding herself about some tall, dark and handsome stranger who would give her a child, then wish her and the baby a fond farewell as they returned to the vagabond life. Since she'd given up on that notion, maybe he stood a chance of changing her belief that she was destined to wander for the rest of her life, as well.

In the wee hours of the morning, he had finally come to grips with what had been happening to him over the past month. Slowly but surely he'd fallen in love with her, and the knowledge that come spring she was going to leave him was tearing him apart. As well as the most beautiful, Serena was the most caring person he'd ever run across, unreservedly generous with her time and energies. Along with her tonics and tinctures, she passed out equal measures of laughter and compassion. Her love of life seemed boundless, and that joy spilled over onto everyone she met.

Sometimes Robert thought of her as a shiny moonbeam that had danced into his life and heart and mind but would soon disappear just like quicksilver. Somehow, he had to convince her to stay. But how did a man capture a moonbeam without destroying all its glowing magic?

"Really, Robert," Serena insisted, concerned by the deep frown on his face. "I don't believe in Grannie's nonsense any longer. If I had been thinking clearly at the time, I never would have believed her in the first place. I knew better than anyone that Grannie's second sight wasn't half as developed as she tried to make other people think."

She was gazing at him with that seductive sparkle in her eyes that he hadn't seen for so long, and Robert responded with an enthusiastic burst of energy. Leaning sideways, he scooped her onto his lap, then stood up with her in his arms and headed for the bed. Once there, he laid her carefully across the mattress and leaned over her. "This is your last chance to say no, Serena."

Serena reached up and slid her arms around his neck, pulling his head down to hers. "This is your last chance to say yes, Robert," she whispered. "I've already admitted what I want. You're the one who keeps holding back."

Holding back nothing, Robert took her lips in a kiss that stole the breath from her body. As the delicious tremors shook her, Serena sank back against the pillows, glorying in the power she seemed to have over him. With each touch of her hands over his muscled back, his breathing became more rapid, until his heartbeat matched hers. "I love touching you, Robert."

Within seconds they were both naked, and Robert was blazing a fiery path of kisses from the hollow of her throat to the valley between her breasts. "And I love tasting you," he murmured as his mouth opened over her nipple.

"Oh, yes," Serena whispered, everything in her rising up in feverish response as he circled her nipple with his tongue, then suckled. "Now I remember why I liked this part so much."

Robert smiled at the eagerness in her voice, the uninhibited pleasure she took in everything he did to her. Her joyful delight was like an aphrodisiac to him, urging him to provide her with more to enjoy so that he could achieve an even greater sense of gratification. Using his mouth and hands and body, he caressed every inch of her satiny skin, explored every curve, until she was gasping in ecstasy.

"Stop! This isn't fair," Serena cried out as the wondrous sensations became almost too much to bear. "Robert, I want to give you the same amount of pleasure you give me."

"Just seeing you like this fills me with pleasure," Robert assured her, but Serena wasn't going to allow him to be content with so little when he gave her so much.

"No, it's my turn now," she insisted as she pressed kisses across his chest and pulled teasingly at a tuft of hair. She laved his nipple with her tongue then drew the tight point into her mouth. Robert flinched, and she looked up at him swiftly. "Did I hurt you?"

"Hurt me again," he pleaded thickly, his throat so dry he could barely talk.

She repeated the entire process, exploring his warm, firm flesh with her fingers, as he'd explored hers. Robert groaned when she slipped her hands lower and blatantly caressed him until he shuddered with the strength of his arousal. He felt himself throbbing all over with a pleasure he could no longer bear.

Grabbing her wrists, he growled, "Now we're even." Then, after reaching into his jeans pocket for protection, he drew her slowly forward, penetrating her with one smooth thrust.

Serena's throat arched as she drew back her head, digging her nails into his shoulders as the fiery rhythm began. She felt as if Robert were binding her to him by electric cords of sensation as an incredible tension flowed through him into her. All at once she was free to soar, but even in flight he was with her, and he was there waiting when she floated back to earth.

"This is one of those times when I wish that the snow would never melt completely," Robert whispered, brushing her hair away from her temples so he could gaze into her eyes.

Remembering the words she'd used when she'd told him his fortune, Serena smiled. "And if the stars deem it right, you will have your heart's desire."

"Then I thank my lucky stars," Robert exclaimed huskily. "Especially if they're responsible for bringing you here to me."

Serena couldn't resist teasing him for that bit of whimsy. "Robert! Do you actually believe that man's fate is written in the stars? How very immature of you."

"Do you mean to say that the fortune you told me was just so much stuff and nonsense?" Robert demanded, trying to appear properly indignant.

Serena gave a tiny, provocative wiggle. "Does it feel like nonsense?"

"Not at all," Robert groaned as the shock of sensation between their still-merged bodies jolted up his spine. "You've just made me a believer."

"I've never put up a Christmas tree before," Serena said conversationally as she helped Robert and Harold carry boxes of decorations into the spacious living room at Laurel Glen. "And this one's so big."

Robert had looked up at the twenty-foot spruce that he and Harold had labored all morning to drag into the house and install beneath the vaulted ceiling. After several hours of backbreaking effort, the tree now stood erect before the huge bay windows, making it visible to anyone who turned into the circular drive. This was his first Christmas at Laurel Glen and he hadn't been aware of the customs the Eastern branch of the family had followed for generations. Since he would be spending the holiday in Montana, Robert still hadn't seen any purpose in putting up a tree but he'd quickly found out that Harold Rutgers and Eugenia Riley had other ideas.

Apparently the Armstrong Christmas tree was considered as much a tradition to the village of Tewksberry as the large plastic candles and red garland that decorated the light posts down Main Street. According to Eugenia, each year's tree brought carloads of viewers from the surrounding township, which meant that not only the tree had to go up, but that hundreds of tiny Christmas lights had to be hung along the drive. The Armstrongs of Laurel Glen had done things exactly this way for as long as anyone could remember, and so it would be done this year if Eugenia had anything to say about it, which she certainly had.

"That thing is going to require gallons of water to stay fresh," Robert remarked. "Who's going to water it while I'm gone?"

Four voices accepted the job at the same time.

Robert expressed his surprise to Betty first. "Don't you have some place else to go for Christmas?"

"Not this year," Betty told him. "I usually go to my brother in New York, but he and his wife are spending Christmas in Europe."

"Harold?"

The elderly man shrugged his shoulders. "As long as my Bluebell has a warm stall and few lumps of sugar in her feed bag, she don't care where we are for Christmas."

"Mrs. Riley?"

"*My* place is here," the lady replied haughtily.

Robert nodded, beginning to wonder if his place wasn't here, too. Although unrelated to any of them, he'd begun to think of these people as part of his family. Over the past two years, Betty Sallinger had become like an older sister to him, and, as difficult as the other two were to handle sometimes, they'd still managed to grow on him. And then there was Serena.

"You're planning to be here, too, aren't you?"

Serena shook her head positively and extended an invitation to the others. "Since Robert will be away, the four of us can celebrate Christmas together down at my cabin."

Her invitation was readily accepted by everyone, and Robert felt even more left out. "You don't have a lot of room down there, not even enough space to put up a tree," he pointed out childishly, but Serena's enthusiasm remained undaunted.

"Good company is all that's necessary to have a happy Christmas," she informed him. "The place doesn't matter. Grannie and I spent a part of our winters at a campsite in the backwoods of Georgia. The same people showed up there every year, and we always celebrated Christmas together. We never bothered with a tree, but on Christmas Eve we enjoyed a beautiful feast and sang and danced beneath the stars."

"Fellow gypsies?" Robert asked, not knowing what other kind of people would be camping outdoors at Christmas.

"Fellow wanderers," Serena supplied vaguely as she opened the top box of the stack she'd placed on the plush eggshell-blue carpeting and gazed with delight at a tiny glass angel with silver-and-gold wings. The box contained a full dozen of the exquisite creations, and she couldn't wait to see what they looked like dangling from the fragrant branches of the stately spruce. Exuberantly she set the first box aside and opened the second, unaware of the three pairs of eyes staring at her.

Urged on by Harold and Betty's silent prompting, Robert asked, "What kind of wanderers?"

Setting aside a layer of yellowed tissue paper, Serena said, "Mainly kings and queens of the road."

"Bums," Harold grunted under his breath, using the poker to jab at the burning logs in the fireplace.

"Hobos!" Robert exclaimed more loudly, exchanging a quick look with Betty, who was stringing holly over the fireplace mantel. "You celebrated Christmas with a bunch of vagrants?"

"Oh, how lovely!" Serena said, ignoring Robert's astonished exclamation as she held up one of the hand-painted glass bulbs she'd discovered inside the next box. "I hope there's more of these."

"None exactly like that," Mrs. Riley informed her, an affectionate smile on her face as she reentered the room carrying a tray of mulled apple cider. "Each box holds a dozen different decorations collected by the family over the years. For example, that red wooden one over there on the couch dates back to before the Civil War, and that black lacquered one was brought over from Scotland by Lachland Armstrong in 1836."

"No kidding!" Distracted for the moment from Serena's amazing account of her past Christmases, Robert located the red box and lifted up the hinged lid.

Inside was a set of hand-carved wooden ornaments, each one different. Among them were a hand-painted image of St. Nicholas wearing somber clothes and an odd pointed hat, a very realistic looking reindeer, a tiny wreath and a Christmas caroler holding a minuscule wooden songbook, embossed with the words *PEACE ON EARTH*.

"Now you can see why this tree means so much to everyone," Eugenia said.

"Yup, anyone viewing the Armstrong tree is in for a treat," Harold said, concurring with Eugenia's feelings on the subject. "Some of them antique decorations are priceless. The year Kerry's folks died, a few ladies from the historical society came by and tried to get her to donate them all for that scraggly excuse for a tree they put up in the town square. Said it was her civic duty to display them to the public."

"Isn't that the most ridiculous idea you ever heard?" Eugenia harrumphed. "Why they would have all been stolen ten minutes after they'd been hung."

Since Betty was a lifetime member of the society, she didn't want to bad-mouth others in the membership, but she had to agree. "That *was* a bad idea, but I would like to have them for the museum, Robert. We could keep them in a locked case until they're needed for Christmas."

"That would be fine with me," Robert said, his eyes narrowed on Serena's face as she gazed with a child's delighted rapture at the matchless decorations. Even something so simple as decorating a Christmas tree was a new and thrilling experience for her, Robert realized, swallowing the sudden lump in his throat. It took so very little to please her.

Clearing his throat, he excused himself from the room. "I'll be right back."

"Is something wrong, Mister Robert?" Eugenia inquired in concern.

"No," Robert said. "I just need to make a phone call."

Closing the door behind him, Robert entered his study and walked swiftly over to the phone on his desk. A minute later he was talking long-distance to his sister-in-law, who was going into her eighth month of pregnancy. His brother Steven was a very lucky man, for, when he'd married Samantha Charles, he'd not only gained himself two fine young sons and a small, lovely daughter, but was now in the process of adding a fourth to his happy family. "I imagine you're as big as a house by now, Samantha."

"You've got that right, Robert!" Samantha exclaimed happily. "We were wondering when we were going to hear from you. Have you made your flight arrangements yet?"

"Not yet," Robert lied, looking up the number for his travel agent while he talked. "That's what I called about. There's been a snag in my plans. Is the proud papa around?"

Steven must have been listening on an extension, for he was the one who answered. "What kind of snag are we talking about here, Rob? The valuable four-legged kind in your barn or the two-legged variety in your bedroom?"

Robert rolled his eyes at the phone, wondering if the day would ever come when his big brother wouldn't be able to read him like a book. "I've met someone, Steven," he admitted. "And she's all alone in the world."

"Oh, brother," Steven groaned. "Samantha, have I ever told you about Robert's hobby?"

"No, I don't believe you have," Samantha said with laughter in her voice.

"Well," Steven began, "ever since he's been a little kid he's been taking in strays. One year he'd fill the henhouse full of birds with broken wings and the next he'd be hand-feeding a bunch of helpless wolf pups that had lost their mother. Then—"

Robert interrupted before Steven could continue in what he knew was a very long list. "Since this is *my* nickle, let's forego the rest of this litany for another time. Samantha, I'm sorry I can't make it this year," he apologized. "Please hug the kids for me, and tell them that I'll get their presents in the mail today."

"We'll all miss you, Rob," Samantha said, giving him no further argument.

Surprisingly, Steven didn't, either, but wished him an affectionate merry Christmas. "And if this woman turns out to be the right one, we expect to be the first to know."

"As soon as I know, you'll know," Robert promised, then said goodbye before Steven started plying him with questions for which he didn't have answers. At this point all he did know was that he wanted to be with the woman he loved at Christmas, especially since it might be the only one they would ever share.

Six

Wishing that he'd never introduced the subject, Robert gazed over at the beautifully naked woman who occupied the other half of his antique Colonial bed. "You were feeling sorry for me?" Serena laughed, her eyes twinkling. "Oh, Robert, you're such a softhearted person, but this time your concern was misplaced. Christmas for me was like a festive week-long party."

When she'd first told him about the way she'd spent her past holidays, Robert had formed a pathetic picture of her as a young child, crouched around an open fire with others as destitute as herself, sharing a meager dinner of canned beans and hobo soup, but Serena completely dispelled that notion. "I had the time of my life. Most kids are happy with whatever Santa Claus happens to bring them. But every year I looked forward to ten-to-twenty Santa Clauses all to myself, and they brought me special gifts from all over the country."

"I still think you were deprived," Robert insisted, but he didn't sound half as convinced as he had when they'd begun this conversation. In fact, he was beginning to feel somewhat foolish, especially when he heard the indulgent tone in Serena's voice as she set him straight. At times she made him feel as if *he* were the young, inexperienced one in this relationship, and she the old and wise.

"I wasn't deprived of a thing," Serena continued, her face lit up in memory. "Every child looks forward to the time they can open their presents, but the days before Christmas were even more exciting for me because I never knew who was going to get off the train or what they were going to bring me, and everyone brought me something."

"What kind of somethings?"

Serena cocked her head to one side, thinking back to Christmas days that were so different from the one she'd just experienced, days when there was no such thing as tradition, and she'd never known what to expect. "Well, let's see . . . Injun Pete usually arrived first, and since he claimed to be the chief of some long-lost tribe, he'd present me with an Indian poncho or a corn husk doll or a pair of beaded moccasins."

Grinning at Robert's wide-eyed expression, she continued, "Then there was Big Daddy Johanson, who was always hoping to strike it rich in Atlantic City. He usually made me a rock-candy necklace that

I could both wear and eat, or some saltwater taffy. None of those hobos, as you called them, had much money, but they made sure I had the best Christmas any child could have."

"It *does* sound like you had fun," Robert had to admit. "But you never even had a Christmas tree."

"I was surrounded by a whole forest of Christmas trees," Serena corrected. "It just wasn't necessary for me to decorate them. As Grannie used to say, Mother Nature did a much better job of it than any of us could ever do, so why bother? It rarely snowed that far south, but some mornings the trees would be coated with a hoary frost. Then, when the sun came up, every pine needle would look like it was diamond coated. I don't think I've ever seen a lovelier decoration on a tree than a pinecone tipped with sparkling frost."

Robert remembered how the forests surrounding the Triple A had looked after a fresh snowfall and had to agree.

Serena smiled. "No amount of money could buy what I got to enjoy for free. Those colorful lights you've got strung up along the drive are very pretty, but they can't compare with the kind of light the moon and the stars provide. At night, when we danced, the moon would change the trees to silver and light up the entire clearing. With a million stars shining down on me, I felt just like a fairy princess, dancing in an enchanted forest."

With her petite body, delicate features and silvery-gold hair, she looked like a fairy princess, and Robert was the one who felt enchanted. "Stay with me tonight, Serena. All night,'' he murmured, praying she would be willing to break the rules for once.

Up until now, she'd been so adamant about maintaining her independence from him that he hadn't even dared ask, afraid he would get the same kind of answer he'd gotten when he'd offered her a job helping Mrs. Riley around the house. He could still recall the sparks of temper shooting from her eyes as she'd haughtily informed him that she was doing quite well for herself without his help and would continue to do so long after she'd left Laurel Glen. Being a Drabarnie was her vocation, not just a job, and she would follow her natural calling no matter what kind of salary Rob was willing to offer.

"I'm not asking you to make any commitments," he added grimly when Serena remained silent.

It seemed like an eternity to him before she came to a decision and snuggled down beneath the quilts. "Spending the night with you here would be the perfect ending for this perfect day."

With a sigh of relief, Robert slid down beside her, then drew her into his arms until her head was resting back against his bare shoulder. Still replete from their last session of lovemaking, he was willing to forego the next for a short while longer. It felt so good just to hold her and know that he would wake up tomorrow with her still in his arms.

Actually the whole day had been good, Robert admitted. "Even Mrs. Riley seemed to enjoy herself."

"She's in her glory when someone compliments her cooking, and between you and Harold, there was hardly anything left of her roast goose and chestnut stuffing.''

Considering the amount of food he'd packed away today, Robert was surprised that he could still move, but that didn't stop him from saying, ''Next year she'll have to order a bigger bird.''

Instantly he was aware that he'd said the wrong thing, at least from Serena's point of view. He'd referred to a time when they might no longer be together, and, according to the sudden stiffness in her body, she didn't like thinking about that any better than he did. Her reaction made him want to shout for joy. For the first time in days, he felt as if he were making progress, and, since spring was many weeks away, there was still time for him to make more.

Glancing down, he noticed that Serena's fingers were closed tightly around the gold locket he'd given her for Christmas, and his confidence grew. Several times today he'd seen her open the small heart and gaze lovingly at his picture. When the time came maybe she would decide that she would rather have the real thing than settle for a photo.

With that thought in mind, he tilted up her chin and gave her a kiss worth remembering, the first of many he planned to deliver before morning.

Serena slipped out of bed at dawn and swiftly got dressed. From the moment she'd first opened her eyes and looked over at the man sleeping contentedly beside her, all she could think about was getting away, breaking free of the sensual bonds that tied her to him, before they became too strong to break.

Trying not to make a sound, Serena crept out of the room and down the winding staircase. Ignoring the portraits of Robert's ancestors that hung on the walls, she passed swiftly through the long entry hall. Moments later she was standing outside on the front portico, breathing in huge gulps of cold air, hoping the shock would reduce the sense of panic and guilt she was feeling. It seemed as though her thoughts were all jumbled together inside her brain, a tangle of confusion that kept getting worse the longer she stayed at Laurel Glen.

She'd been raised to cherish her freedom, yet the thought of belonging to someplace appealed to her in a way she'd never expected. Last night, however, she'd accepted the fact that the place didn't have nearly the hold on her heart as did the man. She'd fallen in love with Robert Armstrong, thoroughly, completely in love, and she was going to have to suffer the consequences of that mistake for the rest of her life. Yesterday she'd indulged herself in the fantasy of being a cherished part of Robert's family, of belonging in his magnificent house and in his bed, but this morning she was faced with the grim reality of her situation.

All she needed was one glance at the portraits of the other women who had once lived in his house to tell her that she didn't belong to Robert and never could. Robert was a man who put down roots, and the deeper they grew, the happier he became. She, on the other hand, had always felt that her happiness was based on the unlimited adventures that could be found down the road, perhaps around the very next corner.

Robert's goal was to make Laurel Glen into a showplace for Thoroughbreds, and to accomplish that goal, he needed a wife of high social standing to be mistress of his house, a sophisticated woman who could claim the same kind of superior breeding as his horses. Serena had no such breeding or social standing. She would never fit in here.

She'd been naive to even entertain the possibility that she could make Robert an acceptable wife. He certainly hadn't considered it. Before asking her to spend the night in his house, he'd told her that he wasn't asking for any commitments. It had been a warning, but she'd deluded herself into thinking he was catering to her needs, not his own. Luckily the euphoria that had clouded her thinking all day yesterday had completely dissipated by this morning. No matter who she pretended to be, a gypsy she was, and a gypsy she would stay.

It was time to move on.

By midmorning, Robert had eliminated the major highways and was concentrating his search on the back roads. He didn't know exactly how long Serena had been gone, but he figured it couldn't have been more than a few hours. A horse-drawn wagon couldn't get very far in that amount of time, but not knowing which direction Serena had taken, or which road she was on, made it difficult to find her.

"But I will," Robert vowed quietly. "And when I do..."

* * *

On a winter's day in New England, the sun dropped
very quickly from the sky, and the late-afternoon
shadows crossing the tree-lined road made it difficult
to see what lay ahead. There was no wind. Not even
the tops of the trees were moving, but the air was bit-
terly cold, and the temperature was steadily drop-
ping.

For the past several miles, Serena had searched for
a likely shelter for her horse, but thus far she'd found
nothing suitable. She should have figured on having
this problem, but she hadn't been thinking about poor
William's well-being when she'd started out this
morning. She'd only been thinking about her own.

She should have headed toward New York City and
civilization, but instead she'd headed due west, into an
upland terrain broken by numerous gorges and narrow valleys. Unfortunately for her horse, her wish to
avoid people meant doing without those things people left in their wake, like abandoned farms, houses
and barns. It was beginning to look as if she would
have to construct a makeshift shelter for William, for
it was growing dark and time to make camp.

Less than a mile later, Serena spotted a break in the
tress and pulled off the road. Since her caravan trailer
included everything she would need for the night, her
first order of business was to see to her horse's needs.
She and her grandmother hadn't done much winter
camping, but they'd always been prepared for any type
of weather. Going to the back of her trailer, she pulled
out a canvas tarp, a rope and three large horse blankets.

Familiar with the task, it didn't take her long to string the rope between some trees and devise a three-sided tent. Draping the tarp over the top to accommodate William's height was a bit more difficult, but she managed it by climbing up on one of the lower branches. Over the winter the horse had grown a warmer coat, and now that he was protected from the wind, he would weather the night just fine.

After rubbing him down, Serena fetched some water from the stream running nearby and filled his feed bag. Once that was done, she went in search of firewood and luckily found some dead branches that weren't too wet to burn. As soon as she had the camp fire going, she went back to the trailer to fetch the supplies she needed to make herself a meal. She was still warm from the exertions of setting up camp, but it was going to be a cold night, and she wanted to get inside the caravan as quickly as possible after eating.

Robert couldn't believe his luck when he drove around a curve in the winding graveled road and his headlights glanced off the gaily painted side of Serena's caravan. If it had been parked any farther off the road, he would have missed seeing it, but it looked as if the Fates had decided to give him a break. All day long he'd driven up one road and down another, imagining the worst kind of calamity that might have befallen Serena, but at last he'd found her, and she was apparently safe and sound.

"But she won't be once I get through with her," Robert growled as he drew his car to a halt and got out several yards ahead of where the caravan had turned off the road. Walking back toward the narrow break in the trees, he pulled up the collar of his sheepskin jacket and thrust his bare hands into the pockets to keep them warm. His anger grew to major proportions when he stumbled down a slippery incline and spotted a camp fire and the slender figure seated before it.

As if it were the middle of summer instead of the dead of winter, Serena was seated on a blanket she'd placed over the snow-packed ground, holding a stick over the fire and roasting what looked like a hotdog. The damned fool woman wasn't even wearing a coat, but was lounging around on what was bound to be one of the coldest nights of the year in a sweatshirt and a thin pair of jeans!

Instead of being frightened by the shadowy figure stalking toward her, Serena looked up and emitted a defeated sigh. "You shouldn't have come after me, Robert. It would have been better for both of us if you'd forgotten I ever existed."

After the day he'd just put in, Robert was in no mood for a rational discussion. "Sometimes I wish I *could* forget," he snarled as he reached down and hauled her up by her wrists. "And believe me, this is definitely one of those times."

Glaring down into her face, he ranted, "After this ridiculous escapade, I shouldn't give a bloody damn about you, especially since it proves just how little you care about me. But I *do* care, dammit! And I've been through hell today wondering where you were and if you were all right."

"I care about you, too," Serena cried, not even attempting to struggle out of his steely grip. The firelight cast flickering shadows over the planes of his face, making him look quite savage, she saw his pain in his glittering eyes. "I care very much."

With a jerk, Robert pulled her against him, as if needing to punish her as much as he needed to confirm that she was alive and unhurt. "Then how could you do this to me, Serena? If you care so damned much, how could you pack up and leave me without even saying goodbye?"

"Because I've fallen in love with you, Robert," Serena replied truthfully.

As usual, Robert was completely taken aback by her honesty and stunned by her unexpected admittance. "Wha...what did you say?" he demanded gruffly.

"I love you," Serena repeated sadly. "That's why I had to leave and why I can't go back."

Later he would get to the bottom of that idiotic conclusion, but right now all Robert could think about was the joy he felt at her disclosure.

"Oh, God," he groaned, wrapping his arms around her waist and lifting her up off her feet. "I love you, too. I could've died when I woke up and found you gone." And then he was kissing her as if he would never stop.

Serena tried to resist, but it was useless, for her own body was his strongest ally. As she melted into his arms, his lips took possession of the soft mouth he now considered his own personal property, renewing the claim he'd staked on her the night before. With sweet aggression his tongue pressed for welcome, and she gave it, opening to him until she was filled by his taste.

Serena knew that this was the last time she would ever kiss him, the last time she would feel Robert's strong body so close to hers, and she wanted to savor every minute of the pleasure. Her need for him was elemental, her wanton response to his kisses proclaiming something she'd feared all along.

Grannie Heidi *had* had a vision. She *had* seen the man who could make Serena profoundly happy, and that man was indeed Robert Armstrong. He was her mate, physically, spiritually, in all ways, just as Grannie had predicted. Serena belonged to him and he to her, but what Grannie's vision had failed to show was that they would only have this short time to spend together, for, no matter how much they cared about each other, she would never fit into his world, nor he into hers.

Before things got completely out of hand and they ended up making love in the frigid outdoors, Robert reluctantly drew away from her. "Come on. Let's get out of here before we both catch pneumonia. I passed a motel before I decided to take this cutoff into the hills. It's only a few miles away. I'll drive your wagon, and you can follow me in the car."

Catching her hand, he started walking toward the enclosure she'd devised for William, but Serena held back. "I'm not going back with you, Robert. Loving each other isn't enough. My future lies down this road or the next one or the one after that, but yours is waiting for you back at Laurel Glen."

A blast of cold air cut across the clearing, and Robert felt Serena shiver as a flurry of snowflakes swirled up around them. "Our futures lie together," he stated resolutely, scowling when she stood firm. "For God's sake, Serena, now's not the time to stand around and argue about this. I realize we've got a few problems that will need working out, but it's getting colder every second, and you're not even wearing a coat. Show some sense, will you?"

"The problems we have can never be worked out," she informed him, fighting back tears. "So if you don't mind, I'd rather we said our goodbyes right now. Dragging it out will only make the parting more painful."

Under other circumstances Robert would have attempted to be more sympathetic to her feelings. Serena was spouting nonsense, but it was obvious that her distress was serious and genuine. Unfortunately, the falling temperature was just as real, and the consequences could be deadly serious if they stayed outdoors much longer. "Do you want to walk to the car, or should I carry you?"

"I'm staying here, Robert," Serena insisted stubbornly.

"Okay," Robert said, moving so quickly that Serena didn't have a chance to react as he scooped her up into his arms and started walking. "Have it your way."

"I'm not going with you!" Serena cried, trying to wiggle out of his hold.

"So you said," Robert agreed as he pulled open the door of her trailer, set her down on her feet inside, then climbed inside himself. "Damn, Serena!" he swore, as he pulled the door shut behind him. "It's almost as cold in here as it was out there."

The interior of the caravan was also pitch-black, and Robert tripped over something and fell forward before Serena could light the lamp. Once she did, she couldn't help laughing, for Robert was sprawled face-down on her narrow cot, and a heap of her clothing had fallen on top of him from the cupboard above it. As he struggled to get out from beneath the mound, she chided, "Serves you right, Robert Armstrong. I didn't invite you in here."

Casting a fluffy sweater away from his eyes, Robert retorted, "Well, you'd better get used to the idea, because if you're staying, I'm staying."

"Suit yourself," Serena said, deciding not to debate the issue. Robert could be just as stubborn as she was, and perhaps spending the night in her caravan would do more to convince him that they weren't destined to be together than anything she could say. He was a big man, and these were very cramped quarters, for life on the road demanded the efficient use of space. By the time this night was over, there was a very good chance that he would reach the same conclusion she'd reached earlier today. The vagabond life was not for him, any more than his life was for her.

Reaching into a wooden box lashed to the side wall, Serena found a box of matches. She could feel Robert's eyes on her as she opened the bottom grate in the small kerosene heater placed near the back door, but when she lit a match, she was unprepared for his reaction. "Are you crazy! Do you want us to asphyxiate?" he shouted, bumping his head on the ceiling as he tried to stand up. "Or would you rather we died in a fire?"

Pushing open the vent cut into the wall above the heater, Serena scoffed at his concern. "With the proper ventilation, there's no danger."

"The hell there's not," Robert blazed. A fast learner, he didn't make any sudden moves, but edged himself carefully down to the end of the cot. Then, using one arm to close the damper on the heater and the other to close the vent, he settled the matter.

"You're not burning that thing while I'm in here," he stated grimly but didn't add that she wouldn't be burning it even when he wasn't. Serena wasn't too pleased with him at the moment, and he didn't want to press his luck, but just thinking about the risks she'd been taking for God knew how long made him shudder. She didn't know it yet, but she wouldn't be taking such chances again.

"How do you expect to stay warm now?" Serena demanded in frustration before reading the answer in his eyes. "Oh, no, we're not sharing the same cot. It's not big enough for two people. I'm sleeping on the other one."

"Where I come from, the temperature can go to fifty below zero in the blink of an eye. One of the first things a man learns when he gets stranded in the cold is how to benefit from shared body heat."

Serena backed up until her shoulder blades were pressed against the door, but she took too long fumbling with the lock to do herself any good. With one sweep of his arm, Robert had her around the waist, and a second later she was lying flat on her back on the cot with Robert lying on top of her.

"And this isn't a very good idea, either," Robert said, leaning over to blow out the lamp. "If you want light, get something that's battery operated."

What followed was a silent fight in the cold and the dark that Serena inevitably lost. "You're a...you're a..." she sputtered at him from inside the sleeping bag, unable to think of any name bad enough.

Robert filled in the blanks himself. "I'm the man who loves you and won't let you catch your death of cold," he said, and turned over onto his side so her naked body was curled spoon fashion in front of his. Serena squirmed for release, then gasped as a large warm hand closed over her breast and another settled firmly over her stomach.

"The last time I was forced to share a sleeping bag, it was with Con," Robert said, laughter rumbling in his chest. "We got trapped up on Bear Claw Mountain during a snowstorm, and it was either that or freeze to death." Capturing her nipple between his fingers, he continued, "I think I'm going to enjoy this much better. Not only did Con snore, but every time he rolled over, I was left out in the cold."

Robert had told her all about Conlan Fox, the part Absaroka Indian who had grown up with him. Upon learning that Rob and Con were blood brothers, as well as best friends, Serena had understood why Robert had been so ashamed of himself for the prejudice he'd displayed toward her the day they'd met. Normally she enjoyed listening to the stories Rob had to tell her about his rollicking boyhood adventures with Con and Rob's older brother Steven, but tonight wasn't one of those times.

"Stop that," she ordered, trying to trap his caressing hands with her own before they wandered any lower. For a few seconds she managed to halt his exploration, but her satisfaction in the accomplishment didn't last long. In her efforts to keep him from arousing her beyond the point of no control, she'd pushed him to the limits of his.

Feeling her buttocks pressed tightly against his throbbing sex, Robert groaned, and the sheer urgency of his need inspired an equal need in her. She loved him, and this was the last night they would ever be together like this, her last chance to feel the glorious wonder that came with their every joining.

"Make love with me, Serena," Robert pleaded, and she complied, but not like he expected. Knowing she might never see him again, Serena wanted to please him in a way she'd never dared before, and so she pulled down the heavy zipper and twisted around until her body was facing his.

When her mouth met the flatness of his belly, it was Robert's turn to emit a startled gasp, but when he felt her lips slide even lower, he forced himself to lie perfectly still. He'd loved her this way before, but this was the first time she'd attempted to emulate what he'd taught her. "Oh, lord, Serena," he groaned as her soft mouth claimed him. "I don't know if I can stand this."

"If I can, you can," she whispered, the heat of her breath adding to the already unbearable pleasure. It might be the coldest night of the year, but Robert felt as if he were on fire, and Serena was the flame. The brush of her silvery-blond hair across his burning skin was an exquisite torment, and the ardor of her lips, fevered torture.

On the brink of release, Robert grabbed for her in an attempt to regain control, but Serena refused to relinquish it. Rising to her knees, she straddled him and sheathed his masculine power inside herself with one undulating motion. As she established their rhythm, Serena gazed down into her lover's face, grateful for the shaft of moonlight that filtered through the window, highlighting his handsome features and the muscular contours of his naked body.

As long as she lived, Serena would never forget how he looked in the silvery moonlight, lost in the throes of passion she alone had inspired. She would hold on to this beautiful memory, and it would sustain her through the long, lonely nights to come. Turning her own face into the light, Serena closed her eyes, unable to hold back as the wondrous sensations gathered inside her. Together with the man she loved, she soared higher and higher and then... with one final burst of ecstasy, the memory was complete.

Seven

"I don't believe this!" Robert growled in frustration as he rolled off the cot. "After the incredible night we just shared, how can you sit there and tell me you're not going back with me?"

"I knew you'd never understand," Serena sighed miserably. "That's why I left without telling you in the first place."

"What's to understand?" Robert demanded, bending over so he wouldn't hit his head on the ceiling as he pulled on his jeans. "Your logic is idiotic."

"I'm only doing what I think is best for both of us."

"Well, think again!" It was so cold inside the caravan Robert could see his breath, but he didn't feel it. The heat of his temper was more than enough to keep him warm. "And this time don't give me that bit about not being good enough for me. You've never been impressed by the size of my wallet, so don't expect me to buy that.''

"It doesn't have anything to do with your money," Serena insisted. "It has to do with the kind of social circles you move in."

Robert glared at her. "Don't be stupid!"

"I'm not being stupid. I'm being realistic," Serena retorted indignantly as she slid off the end of the cot. Shivering in the frigid morning air, she swiftly got into her underwear, then reached into the cupboard built over the cot and removed a heavy sweater and a pair of woolen pants. "And I never said I wasn't good enough for you."

"That's sure what it sounded like," Robert contradicted, thrusting his arms into his plaid flannel shirt as he quoted her. "'I'm a no-account gypsy, Robert. What kind of mistress would I make for Laurel Glen?'"

With a snort of disgust he challenged, "And you accused *me* of being prejudiced? You're the one who seems to have a problem with who you are."

Becoming more defensive every second, Serena tried to restate her position in terms that Robert would find more acceptable. "I didn't mean I'm not good enough for you. I meant that I don't have the same priorities as you do. We want different things out of life."

"What is it you think I want that you don't have to offer?" Robert asked, getting down on his hands and knees to search for his shoes and socks.

With her face hidden by the sweater she was tugging down over her head, Serena replied, "A permanent commitment."

"Uh-huh. At last we're finally getting somewhere," Robert said as he pulled his shoes out from underneath the cot and sat down on the floor to put them on. "You're running scared."

"I am not!"

Ignoring her denial, Robert spoke to her in a soothing tone, as if she were a frightened child. "If a man and a woman love each other, Serena, it's natural for them to want to be together. I realize that the thought of forever is pretty overwhelming, but we'll take it one day at a time. There's no reason to panic."

"I'm not in a panic."

"Then you accept that we were meant to be together?"

"Maybe," Serena hedged, and Robert lost his temper again.

"Maybe!" he exploded. "Either you want to be with me or you don't!"

Serena stepped into her shoes and pulled her jacket off the hook near the door. One of her reasons for leaving Laurel Glen without saying goodbye was to avoid a scene just like this one, but Robert was insisting that they play this out to the bitter end. She didn't want to hurt him any more than she already had, but he wasn't leaving her any choice. "I may want to be with you right now, but I can't promise I'll feel like that tomorrow."

Instead of being hurt by her lack of faith in their relationship, Robert laughed. "You will."

"You may think so, but I'm not that sure."

"I'm willing to chance it."

"Would you really want a woman who can't be certain of her feelings from one day to the next?" she shouted in exasperation.

"You'll be sure," Robert assured her with an arrogance born from the most incredible session of love-making he'd ever endured in his life. Slowly he moved his eyes up her body, his possessive gaze lingering for a moment on her breasts, and Serena's response to that look was instantaneous. Grinning at her flushed face, he continued, "And after we're married, it will be my great pleasure to make certain you stay sure."

"See!" Serena accused, and pushed open the door. "That's exactly what I'm talking about!"

Taken aback by her irate outburst, Robert was slow to react, and she was outside before he could stop her. "What is?" he shouted after her as Serena stomped angrily around the corner of the caravan and out of his sight. Not waiting to put on his jacket, Robert went after her.

"What is?" he repeated when he caught up with her, grasping her shoulder to twirl her around.

Serena attempted to shrug off his grasp, but when he wouldn't let go, she burst out, "Just because I've admitted I love you, you make all the wrong assumptions. For instance, when did I ever say I wanted to get married?"

Enraged by the contemptuous tone in which she posed the question, Robert shouted, "That's what loving a person normally leads to!"

"That's exactly what I mean!" Serena shouted back. "In your world, love and marriage go hand in hand, but in my world it just doesn't work that way."

"Why the hell not?"

"Because I can't change who I am."

Robert stared down into her face. "I don't want to change you, Serena. I just want us to be together."

"But for us to be together, I would have to change," Serena told him. "Marriage to you would mean giving up the freedom I've enjoyed all my life, and I don't want to do that, Robert. Don't you see? I *can't* do that."

Robert dropped his hands from her shoulders, and he stepped back, his face ashen. Last night, instead of convincing her that she belonged with him, the intensity of his lovemaking had made her feel trapped. "Is that how you view my love for you? As some kind of prison?"

Serena closed her eyes to shut out the agonizing pain she saw in his expression. "Not today, Robert," she whispered. "But that's how I might come to feel."

"I see," he murmured so quietly that she almost didn't hear him. When she opened her eyes, he was already turning away. Later she would regret calling him back, but loving him the way she did, she couldn't let it end like this.

Laying her hand on his sleeve, she apologized, "I didn't intend to fall in love with you, Robert, and I never meant to hurt you."

Robert nodded, the censure in his eyes self-directed. "You know what they say about people who make assumptions, Serena, so there's no need for you to feel guilty. I'm the one who jumped to conclusions concerning our future, not you."

Appalled by the pained look on his face, Serena leapt to his defense. "Under the circumstances, the conclusions you jumped to were perfectly logical," she declared, determined to prove that she was the most to blame. "After the way we spent last night, you had every reason to think I'd go back with you today."

For a moment there, Robert had believed that he'd lost her, but she'd just provided him with some hope. As he gazed down into her anguished face, Robert realized that she didn't want to leave him any more than he wanted to go, but feeling the way she did, she didn't see any other option.

Suddenly he knew where he'd gone wrong with her, and he wanted to kick himself. Over the years he'd discovered some pretty surefire methods for taming wild creatures, but when it came to this flighty female, he'd forgotten every lesson he'd ever learned. Instead of employing the tactics that had worked so successfully for him in the past, he'd rushed her into a corner, and all of her instincts were telling her to run.

With a sense of renewed purpose, Robert thought back to the motherless fawn he'd run across when he was a kid, remembering the hours he'd stood in one spot while she'd worked up the courage to come closer and accept his help. It had taken days before that creature had finally trusted him enough to eat out of his hand, and days more before she'd allowed him to pet her without bolting.

Serena was like that fawn, and he had to be patient for as long as it took if he didn't want her to bolt. To capture the heart of his wild little gypsy, he had to let her do the chasing, until he caught her. Putting that theory into practice, he patted the small hand placed on his sleeve, but made no attempt to hold it. "I'm sorry I got so carried away with my own feelings that I didn't take yours into consideration."

"I'm just as guilty of that as you are," Serena maintained. "I knew I was getting in too deep, and I should have done something about it far earlier. I wasn't being honest with you or myself, and the only excuse I have for my behavior is that I loved every minute of our time together, and I didn't want it to end so soon."

"What we had was special—very, very special," Robert agreed tenderly, bending down to brush a soft kiss on the corner of her mouth. "A part of me will always love you, Serena. It's going to take me a long time to forget you."

Yesterday she'd told him that she wanted him to forget that she'd ever existed, but hearing him say that he was going to give it a try hurt her like nothing else ever had. Robert was telling her goodbye, but instead of feeling relief, she felt angry. For a man who'd been talking marriage less than ten minutes ago, he'd certainly switched gears in a hurry. "I . . . I'll never forget you, either."

To keep himself from pulling her into his arms, Robert thrust his hands into the front pockets of his jeans. "So where will you go now?"

Serena frowned, stunned by his sudden capitulation to her viewpoint. "I . . . I'm not sure."

"Maybe you should head south where it gets warm earlier."

"Maybe."

Robert accompanied her to William's enclosure and helped her take down the blankets. "If you have any more of that stuff you mix up for Bluebell, I can take it back with me. I hate to admit it, but it sure seems to help the old nag."

"I'll get you some."

"Great," Robert said, folding up the tarp while she folded the blankets. "And how about that feed mix for my horses. Do you have any more of that?"

"That has to be mixed up fresh every day."

"Oh."

"You wouldn't happen to have another packet of those herbs Mrs. Riley uses in her salads, would you?"

"No."

"What about that tonic for Betty's dog? Does she have enough of that to last her for a while?"

When she'd taken off yesterday morning, the last things on her mind had been Harold's horse or Betty's dog, but now that Robert had mentioned them, she realized that she'd left without saying goodbye to their owners. Harold and Betty had become her dear friends, and then there was Mrs. Riley and Bill Murdock and the exercise boys, all of whom had been so good to her. The least she owed them was an explanation for her abrupt departure, as Robert very well knew.

As she hitched William up to the trailer, Robert reminded her that Huey Stone was still suffering from his sore throat, but that her elixir was helping, confirming her suspicion that he was deliberately preying on her conscience. Casting him a cutting glance, she bit out, "I know what you're trying to do, and it's not going to work."

Robert's brows rose, his face a picture of innocence. "I'm not doing anything."

"Yes, you are," Serena retorted. "You're trying to make me feel guilty for leaving all my friends in the lurch."

Knowing he was taking a great risk, Robert replied, "It's not my fault that so many people rely on you to cure their ailments and treat their pets. You're the one who's responsible for that. As you repeatedly tell me, being a Drabarnie is your calling."

"Do they really rely on me, Robert? Or would they just like me to think so?"

Robert frowned. "What kind of question is that? You know how they all feel about you."

Serena nodded. "Yes, I do. They see me as a poor orphan who couldn't survive without their charity, but I'm a lot tougher than I look. When Grannie was alive, we used to take advantage of people who saw me as a little lost urchin, but I don't want to do that anymore. I want people to respect me for what I know and what I can do for them."

Realizing he'd chosen the wrong method to make his case, Robert tried a different tack. "Respect has to be earned, Serena. How do you expect anyone to get past your looks if you keep moving all the time? You're not giving them a fair chance."

Robert could be right about that, but that wasn't the biggest problem facing her if she went back with him. "You know darned well that if I stay on at Laurel

Glen, you and I will continue exactly where we left off."

"Not exactly, Serena," he said, masking his ela-tion behind a smooth expression. He was painfully aware that she was still wavering. "I'd be lying if I said I didn't want you back in my bed, but if you decide to stay on for the rest of the winter as you'd planned, I wouldn't apply any pressure to make you stay any longer."

"You still don't get it, do you? Loving you is the worst kind of pressure there is, and it's tearing me apart," Serena burst out. "When I'm with you, I start thinking that maybe I can change my life-style, that maybe I can be something I'm not. But that's not possible, Robert. Don't you see? Nobody can do that without destroying themselves."

When it came to Serena, Robert only had so much control, and he lost it when he saw the tears rolling down her cheeks. Pulling her into his arms, he pressed her head down against his shoulder and began strok-ing her silky hair. "I'll never ask you to be something you're not," he assured her. "And I don't want you to change a single thing about yourself. All I want is a little more time to be with the woman I love. Is that so much to ask?"

"I don't know if I can give you that," Serena sobbed, lifting her head and gazing up at him with tear-filled eyes. "If I come back, I might not find the strength to leave you again, and eventually that deci-sion could destroy us both."

She was so sincere in her belief that Robert didn't attempt to dissuade her. He knew there was nothing he could say that would convince her that her fears were groundless. She would have to come to that conclusion herself. Serena was certain that her gypsy blood made it impossible for her to stay in one place for any great length of time, but he was equally certain that she could be happy as his wife and completely content as the mother of his children.

That certainty sprang from a subject that neither one of them had brought up in today's discussion. Both of them had been aware that he hadn't used any protection last night, yet neither of them had mentioned it. Robert hadn't worried about getting her pregnant because he'd assumed that they were going to get married right away, and he loved the idea of her having his baby. Now he knew that Serena had been operating on an entirely different wavelength. As yet, she didn't believe that she could be his wife, but she desperately wanted his child even if she couldn't have him.

Serena wasn't going to mention the possibility that she was pregnant for fear that he would force her to stay, and Robert didn't, for fear that it would force her to run, but that awareness was there for both of them. "When spring comes, I'll help you find the strength to leave if you still feel the way you do now," he promised her. "If you decide you have to go, I won't do a thing to stand in your way."

"You wouldn't have to do a thing," Serena complained. "All you'd have to do is look at me the way you do."

"Then let's set a deadline," Robert suggested. "And on that day I won't see you or look at you or even talk to you. When the sun goes down, I'll come to your cabin, and if you're not there, I'll know your decision. And whatever it is, I'll accept it. If you're gone, I'll make no attempt to find you.''

Serena wanted to spend more time with him, too, wanted that so very much that she was willing to bear the pain she knew would come with their inevitable parting. And when she left, there was a chance that she might take a part of him with her. Gazing into his eyes, she saw that he was offering her much more than the freedom to leave if that was her choice. Robert knew that she could be pregnant, as well as she did, but this time he would be willing to let her go even if she was carrying his baby.

Just to make sure, she inquired, ''Do I have your word on that, Robert.''

''You have my word, Serena,'' he vowed, a burning intensity in his green eyes. ''If you decide to leave, I'll do nothing to stand in your way.''

''April first then,'' she decreed purposefully. ''I'll make my decision on April first.''

Robert kissed the top of her head. ''Good choice,'' he complimented. ''No day could be more appropriate than April Fool's Day.''

''Maybe I *am* being a fool,'' Serena stated, a resentful edge in her voice. ''But I can't help how I feel, and I'm not going to go along with this if you're playing some kind of silly game with my emotions.''

''If you're a fool, then so am I,'' Robert replied soberly. ''Because if this is a game, I'm going into it knowing that if you lose, so do I.''

* * *

Robert parked the car in the garage and got out to face the crowd gathered in the driveway. He'd barely driven through the front gates when he'd seen Harold chasing after his car, and, by the time he'd reached the garage, both Betty and Mrs. Riley were scurrying out of the house. Before they could ask, he declared, "I found her camped on the old Church Road, about twenty miles from here."

"And you just up and left her there?" Harold demanded irately.

"In this weather!" Mrs. Riley chided.

"Oh, Robert," Betty sighed in disapproval. "How could you let her go? There's nothing out there but endless acres of forest."

"Thank you all very much for your vote of confidence. I really appreciate it," Robert bit out acidly, vexed by their ready condemnation of him.

Before any of them could work up the courage to approach him again, he strode away toward the house. Once inside, he walked into the living room, positioned a chair in front of the bay window and sat down, making sure he could see the front gate through the branches of the Christmas tree.

Since he hadn't removed his heavy jacket, it was obvious that he was planning to go back outside, and that was what tipped off his inquisitors that they might have been a bit hasty in their judgment. "So you *did* manage to convince her to come back. She's on her way now," Betty said, earning herself another scowl from the condemned man.

"We should have known." Chuckling, Harold placed himself on the other side of the tree and looked out. "Of course that little girl would have too much pride to ride back in the car."

"Pride goeth before a fall," Eugenia declared, peering over Harold's shoulder. "I'm sure Robert did his best, but, once she gets here, someone had better give her another good talking to. That child can't just go off on her own like this without telling anybody. I, for one, was worried half to death."

Betty agreed. "I couldn't stand the thought of her being all alone out there in this cold."

"With no more protection than that rickety old wagon," Harold grunted.

Hearing them talk, Robert realized that he wasn't the only one who was guilty of overprotection. Serena brought out those instincts in everybody, and he had better do some fast talking before she arrived. "Listen up, people. Serena isn't a child. She's a grown woman, and she's quite capable of looking after herself. I know she looks like a strong wind would blow her away, but, the fact is, she's spent her whole life on the road, and she knows how to survive. I talked her into coming back, but if we don't want her to take off on us again, we can't keep treating her like a two-year-old."

Betty made the first attempt to understand the purpose behind his testy speech. "Is that why she left?"

Unwilling to disclose the full story, Robert said, "Serena's a free spirit, and she's used to being on her own. We've got to stop smothering her with our affection."

"Smothering her!" Eugenia exclaimed. "Why I never!"

"And we have to stop thinking we know what's best for her," Robert continued. "We might not be able to understand the way she lives, but that doesn't mean it isn't right for her."

"Oh, my," Betty murmured, getting the message.

Harold turned on the irate housekeeper. "You can deny it all you want, Ginny, old girl, but you dang well know we've all been treating Serena like a baby chick who fell out of her mama's nest."

Eugenia tried to say something in her own defense. "But I can't help worrying about her. That poor little thing is so sweet and trusting, and, without a home or a family, I just know she's going to get hurt if somebody doesn't watch out for her."

"Watching out for her is one thing, but none of us has the right to interfere in her decisions," Robert pointed out gently.

Harold's face screwed up in a thoughtful frown. "Think about it, Eugenia," he growled. "Does she really need us so badly, or is it us who need her?"

Already knowing the answer to that question, Robert returned his gaze out the window. Serena had waved for him to go on ahead soon after they'd set off on their return trip, so it would be quite some time yet before she arrived. Like yesterday, he was worried about her having an accident on the roads, but he couldn't express that worry to her. From now on, he had to give her a free hand and pray to God that, come the first of April, she would be willing to hold on to it.

Noting Robert's strained expression, Betty remembered the day she'd warned Serena not to get involved with him. Now it looked as if she may have warned the wrong person. Stepping up beside Robert's chair, she laid her palm down on his shoulder. "You'll have my cooperation, Robert. When Serena gets back, I'll keep my nose out of her business."

"That goes for all of us," Harold said after sending Eugenia a warning glance and receiving a compliant look in return.

Robert nodded, glad to hear that they were all in agreement. Even so, the minutes ticked by, and no one moved away from the window. When the phone rang a half hour later, all four of them jumped. Eugenia hurried out of the room to answer the summons, muttering what everyone else was thinking. "An accident! I just knew it. She's been in an accident."

All eyes were on her as she came back a few moments later, a disgruntled expression on her face. "It's for you, Mister Robert."

"Who is it?" Robert asked, standing up from his chair.

"Your brother."

Wanting more privacy, Robert bypassed the phone in the entry and picked up the call in his study. As soon as he had heard who was calling, he'd gotten a bad feeling in his stomach, and he hoped his anxiety wouldn't come through in his voice. "Good to hear from you, Steven. Did you and Samantha have a nice Christmas?"

"Pretty nice, though it was the concensus among the kids that it would have been nicer if Uncle Rob had shown up."

"I love them, too," Robert replied, striving for a cheerful tone. "I hope you sent my best wishes along to Conlan and Kerry."

"As a matter of fact, you can do that in person."

Robert sank down into the chair behind his desk, the feeling in his stomach going from bad to worse. "Oh? Are they planning to come out here for a visit in the near future?"

"Not Kerry," Steven replied. "Little Jamie came down with a cold, so she stayed behind to look after him."

Robert's fingers clenched the receiver until his knuckles turned white. "So it's just Con that's coming?"

Robert could picture Steven's grin as he replied, "Besides me, you mean?"

When that unsurprising question was greeted by dead silence, Steven teased, "I know you're disappointed that I came alone, but Samantha's too far along to travel."

That announcement inspired a similar response, so Steven drawled, "Yup, Con and I thought it was a good time to drop in and check out your stock. Both of us are in the market for some horses, and of course we'll trust you to sell the best or put us in touch with the top dealers."

"Drop in from where?" Robert demanded, not bothering to comment on the rest of Steven's flimsy excuse for a visit. If he and Con were in the market for some good horseflesh, Rob knew they could find plenty of it in Montana, and they knew that he knew. The real purpose of their visit was to check out the state of his love life, though how they'd arrived at the conclusion that he would welcome the intrusion was beyond him. Aside from that, their timing couldn't have been worse.

Aware that he shouldn't expect a gracious welcome, Steven was happy to inform Rob of his present whereabouts. "At the moment we're in our rooms at the Waldorf, but you can expect to see us later tonight. We're going to rent a car and drive up." After a short pause, he continued, "Con wants to add his two cents worth, Rob. Here he is."

Rob gritted his teeth when Con's amused voice came over the phone. "Steven tells me that you've developed quite an interest in one particular filly. That so, Rob?"

Knowing his denial was useless, Rob still felt compelled to say, "You know me, Con. When has that ever *not* been so?"

"You've got me there," Con replied. "But this one must be pretty special, or you would've been home for Christmas."

"I *was* home for Christmas," Robert retorted. "If you recall, I own Laurel Glen now."

In the background he heard Steven mutter, "What did I tell you?" and he knew he was doomed when Conlan said, "I guess it's true what they say. Home is where the heart is."

"If either of you two guys had any heart," Robert grumbled, "you'd go back where you came from."

Conlan laughed. "Sorry, pal. You know me and airplanes. I'll need some time to recuperate before I get on another one."

"How much time?"

"A couple of days ought to do it," Con said.

Then Steven spoke into the phone before breaking the connection, "We'll see you soon, little brother."

"Damn!" Robert swore as he slammed down the receiver and stomped out of the room. "The last thing I need is the two of them butting in. Once they get started on her, I'll be lucky if Serena sticks around for more than two minutes."

Eight

I am who I am," Serena said to the flamboyant looking woman staring back at her in the mirror. "And if
Steven Armstrong doesn't like it, he can just lump it."

With a defiant toss of her head, she whirled around
and around, her multicolored floral skirt swirling high
around her legs, revealing her flimsy leather sandals
and the cheap gold bracelets she wore around each
ankle. Maybe the red scarf she'd wrapped around her
hair, the low-cut yellow blouse and the large gold
hoops in her ears were taking things a step too far, but
she didn't want there to be any doubt about her heri-
tage. Like it or not, a gypsy was coming to dinner.

When he'd issued her the invitation, Robert had
tried to deny that he was nervous about introducing
her to his older brother Steven and his best friend

Conlan, but why else would he have tacked on that warning for her to behave herself? She'd been highly insulted by that directive, but she hadn't planned to make such a bold statement concerning her identity until Robert had told her that his brother had the tendency to come on too strong at times, and she shouldn't take offense if he asked her a lot of personal questions.

According to Robert, Steven and Conlan had come East on a horse-buying trip. Since Robert hadn't gone home for Christmas, they'd decided to stop in at Laurel Glen before returning to Montana. Serena, however, had learned through Mrs. Riley that there was more to this impromptu visit than that. Apparently something had tipped Steven off to the possibility that Robert was seriously involved with a woman, and he'd come to Laurel Glen for no other reason than to pass judgment on her.

Unlike Robert, who wanted to brush the problem under the table, Serena felt that his family's disapproval of her had to be faced sooner or later, and it might just as well be sooner. It was time Robert understood that the concerns she had about their possible future together weren't products of an overactive imagination. The people he admired and respected most were not going to accept her, and Robert was going to have to decide if he could live with that fact.

Hiding her own trepidation about this meeting behind a layer of exotic makeup, Serena drew a purple-and-gold fringed shawl around her bare shoulders and stepped outside, where Harold was waiting with a car to drive her up to the main house. She expected him to make some comment when she got in beside him, and he didn't disappoint her. "Read any good palms lately, Madame Danvers?"

"Not lately, but no doubt I'll see the back of a few hands tonight."

With an amused chuckle Harold shifted the car into a forward gear. "I've met the gentlemen you're about to impress, and they don't strike me as the kind to backhand a woman. If I were you, I'd be far more worried about Robert's reaction to that getup you've got on. Once he sets eyes on you, he's likely to turn you over his knee."

"Then I'll be forced to curse him with my evil eye, and he'll rue the day he dared to cross a gypsy," Serena scoffed, with a wave of her bejeweled hand.

Harold was still shaking his head over that bit of false bravado when they drove around the last curve and pulled up in front of the house. As Serena opened the door and stepped out, he admitted, "For the first time in my life, I envy that stiff-necked Eugenia. While I'm stuck at home watching some boring old movie on television, she gets to be entertained by a live show."

"Don't feel too bad, Harold," Serena called back over her shoulder. "I predict it will be a brief performance."

From his guard post beside the window, Robert was able to watch as Serena got out of the car and walked around toward the front portico. When he caught sight of what she was wearing, he rolled his eyes in exasperation. After the stupid way he'd set her up for this meeting with Steven, he should have known she would try something like this, but it was too late to do anything about it now.

Before Serena made it halfway up the steps to the door, Robert let the heavy drape fall back into place and turned around to confront the two men sitting behind him on the couch. "If either one of you makes a single snide comment to her, I swear I'll smash your face in."

"Have you developed a hearing problem lately, Steven?" Conlan inquired with amusement as he picked up his snifter of brandy.

"No," Steven replied. "Why do you ask?"

Conlan shrugged. "Since that's about the tenth time your brother's made that threat, I couldn't help but wonder."

"It's more like the twelfth," Steven observed mildly. "I'm dying to see what it is about this lady that inspires such violence. Aren't you?"

With two fingers, Robert rubbed the spot on his forehead that ached the worst. "I could strangle her," he muttered under his breath.

Steven's brows rose as he exchanged looks with Conlan. "I'm getting more concerned about this boy's mental health all the time, Con. He keeps threatening to hurt innocent people."

As a tight-lipped Mrs. Riley escorted a small but splendiferous siren into the room, Con murmured an astonished aside. "Maybe not so innocent."

"Maybe not," Steven agreed as both men stood up from the couch to await introductions. "And maybe I had good reason to stick my nose in where it doesn't belong."

Robert stepped forward to intercept Serena as she sashayed farther into the room, but she neatly managed to avoid him by skirting gracefully around the backside of an upholstered chair. Both of the men who had risen politely at her entrance were dressed casually in sweaters and dark slacks, and both were tall and broad shouldered. She extended her hand to the one with dark brown hair tinged with auburn and the disapproving brown eyes. "You have to be Robert's brother Steven," she declared with false brightness. "He's told me so much about you."

And none of it good, Steven noted in surprise, sending Robert a questioning look. All he got in return was a helpless shrug. In an attempt to make up the ground he'd lost before they'd even met, Steven accepted the tiny hand being offered to him and lifted it to his mouth. Obviously Serena was expecting him to greet her in the manner of royalty, and Steven gallantly obliged.

"My brother hasn't told me nearly enough about you, Miss Danvers," he drawled, his curiosity intensifying when he noted the guarded gleam in her eyes. "I'm looking forward to our getting better acquainted."

"So am I," she replied insincerely, removing her hand from his grasp as quickly as possible.

Steven was taken aback by her cool tone and prickly manner, and he glanced over at Robert again. According to the sparks shooting from his brother's eyes, Steven gathered that Serena was behaving entirely out of character. He also gathered that it was for his benefit. For what reason he couldn't possibly guess, and apparently neither could his brother. The most easygoing member of the family looked fit to be tied.

Very much aware of the stares directed her way, Serena smiled sweetly at the dark-haired man standing next to Steven. Tilting her chin up at a proud angle, she gazed into eyes as blue as her own and wanted to sigh with relief. Ever since Robert had told her about Conlan Fox, she'd felt a certain affinity for him, and, as he returned her gaze, she felt it was well placed.

Serena's greeting to him was several degrees warmer than the one she'd offered Steven. "I'm delighted to meet you, Mr. Fox."

Enchanted by her delicate face and the mixture of mischief and vulnerability he saw in her eyes, Conlan was won over in a matter of seconds. Whatever this provocative little lady was up to, he was more than happy to go along with it. "I'm delighted to meet you, too, and please call me Conlan."

"Conlan." Serena swiftly obliged in the soft, husky tone she normally reserved for Robert, much to his irritation. "And you can call me Serena."

As he lowered his lips over Serena's trembling hand, Conlan decided that whatever Steven thought, this was a wasted trip. Robert's biggest weakness was his soft heart, but it wasn't matched by a soft head. It was true that he'd always had a penchant for taking in strays, and it looked as if this one were going to cause him no end of trouble. But Con was a good judge of character, and this blue-eyed minx was definitely a keeper.

"Would you care for an aperitif, Serena?" Robert took a forceful grip on her elbow and guided her away from Conlan and into the closest unoccupied chair.

Serena waited until he was on his way to the bar before she turned down his offer. "No, thank you, but if there's anything left of that bottle of moonshine I made for you, I'll take a small glass of that."

"Did she say 'moonshine'?" Steven murmured under his breath to Conlan, but Serena heard.

"Didn't Robert tell you? My grandmother and I used to operate a still down in the Smokies," she said with a brilliant smile.

"No, Robert didn't tell me," Steven said, trying and failing to hide his reaction to the news that his brother was involved with a bootlegger. "All he's really told us about you is that you've led an interesting life, and, I must say, it sounds as if you have."

"To some, I suppose my life would appear interesting," Serena said, forcing back the hurt that his last comment had inspired. It wasn't as if she didn't already know that Robert hadn't looked forward to this meeting, but still, the knowledge that he'd told his brother next to nothing about her came as a painful shock. As much as Robert tried to deny it, a part of him must be ashamed of her. Suddenly Serena couldn't wait for this evening to be over.

"Distilling alcohol is perfectly legal," Robert informed Steven, "if you only make enough for your own use."

"If I remember correctly," Conlan put in helpfully, "your mother used to make some pretty potent elderberry wine."

"Potatoes produce a much higher proof, and I only use the best stuff in my elixirs. If I didn't, I'd have a lot of disappointed customers. Just ask Robert's foreman. He can't seem to get enough of my spring tonic," she said defiantly.

"Oh, brother," Robert groaned, as he compared the shocked expression on Steven's face with the smug look on Serena's.

"Dinner is served," Mrs. Riley announced tartly, much to the relief of every person in the room.

Since Conlan was closest to Serena, he offered himself as her escort, and she was more than happy to accept. Smiling radiantly up into his face, she took his arm, deliberately avoiding Robert's gaze as she walked past him. As they stepped through the door, Conlan glanced back innocently over his shoulder as if to say, *Can I help it if my sex appeal is so irresistible to women?*

"After you, Steven," Robert growled irritably, making a sweeping gesture toward the door.

"Why do I get the feeling that this dinner was a bad idea?" Steven inquired as he passed in front of his brother.

"For the same reason I've got the feeling that it's only going to go from bad to worse," Robert predicted.

"Why didn't you tell me she was so damned young?" Steven muttered.

"Her age is the least of my problems," Robert said heavily.

"Do you have any suggestions for a topic of conversation that won't end up with me putting my foot in my mouth?"

"Your guess is as good as mine," Robert said as the two men started down the long hall.

An uncomfortable silence prevailed as they entered the dining room and seated themselves around the beautifully set Louis Quatorze table. Serena watched in seething silence while, as if by some unspoken right, Steven took the chair at the head of the table and Robert sat down at the foot, leaving Serena and Conlan with the two places facing each other on opposite sides.

Determined to lighten the tension in the room, Steven smiled down the table at Serena as soon as Mrs. Riley had finished serving the first course, a creamy asparagus soup. "One thing Robert did tell me about you is that you're into herbal healing."

Without looking up from her soup, Serena retorted, "And he told me that you're into making money."

"Okay, sweetheart, that does it!" Robert slammed down his spoon and stood up from the table. In three strides he was around to where Serena was seated, and, before she realized what he was up to, he was hauling her out of her chair.

"You'll have to excuse us," he apologized as he bent down and hoisted her up over his shoulder. "But Serena and I have another very pressing engagement, and I'm afraid we'll have to leave you now."

"Robert Armstrong! You put me down this very instant!" Serena shrieked, pounding on his back with her fists, but her protests were to no avail. Robert ignored her words and paid scant attention to the blows raining down on his back.

"Please stay and enjoy the rest of your dinner, boys," Robert said as he carried Serena out of the room. "And if we don't see you again before morning, try to enjoy the rest of your evening. You can bet I'm going to."

With a pensive expression on his face, Steven watched their progress until they disappeared up the stairs. He picked up his soup spoon and continued eating. "Well, Con, do you see any reason why we shouldn't cut this trip short and head back home?"

"Not a one," Conlan replied. "Robert seems to be in control of the situation."

Steven nodded. "I don't know why I was worried."

"Me neither," Conlan said. "Robert's had enough experience with gold diggers to recognize one without your help."

"He needed my help with that scheming Lolita who got her claws into him in his senior year," Steven reminded. "He's always been a pushover for a good sob story."

Conlan shrugged. "He's not that naive kid anymore, and, if I recall, he wasn't too happy with your interference even when he was young. He told me later that he was planning to break off with that girl himself if you hadn't stepped in and forced the issue."

"He never told me that!"

"That's because he realizes you get such a charge out of playing big brother."

"I'm not that bad," Steven muttered, knowing he was guilty as charged.

Conlan's lips twitched. "Right, Steven. You always keep your opinions to yourself. That's why we hopped a plane and came out here."

"Even so, I don't understand why in hell Serena thinks I'm such a jerk. So what if I do care about my brother? Why should that put her on the defensive?"

Conlan winced as a door slammed overhead. "I wouldn't worry about it, Steven. Even as we speak, I'm sure Robert is doing his best to correct any wrong impressions she might have about you."

Both men heard a muted crash and the sound of breaking glass as they returned to their dinner. Conlan's grin widened. "And it sounds like she's got quite a few of them."

Steven scowled and went back to eating his soup. As Mrs. Riley brought in the second course, he asked, "Since we're obviously not needed here, how would you feel about taking the red-eye flight out of La Guardia?"

"Sounds good," Conlan agreed, glancing up at the glass pendants of the chandelier that were tinkling together from the vibrations. "I don't know about you, but I'm starting to feel very homesick for my wife."

"Me, too," Steven conceded, digging into his pocket for the keys to their rental car. "I can't think of anything more enjoyable than tangling with a feisty woman."

"And making up afterward."

Steven smiled as he thought of his most recent altercation with Samantha. "Think Rob will understand if we skip the goodbyes?"

Cocking his head to one side, Conlan listened but could hear nothing. "I'm almost certain of it," he said, casting a last longing gaze at the beautiful rolled roast he wouldn't have time to eat.

Steven noted Conlan's wistful expression as he got up from his chair. "C'mon, if we don't leave now, we'll miss our flight. We can get something to eat on the plane."

"Okay," Conlan growled, tossing his napkin down on his empty plate. "But the next time you try and convince me to join you on one of these cock-and-bull rescue missions, you know what answer to expect."

"I've a feeling there won't be a next time," Steven acknowledged sheepishly.

Giving the thumbs-up sign to the ceiling, Conlan teased, "Your sound judgment is one of the things I've always admired most about you, Steven."

* * *

Robert set Serena down on her feet and turned around to lock the door to his bedroom. "Of all the childish, uncalled-for displays I've ever witnessed," he began, but his litany was cut off as a vase went whizzing by his head and crashed into the door. "Dammit, Serena! You're really asking for it!"

Enraged beyond control, Serena ignored his warning and picked up another missile from his nightside table. Unfortunately, before she could launch the ivory hairbrush at Robert's head, she was hit by a flying tackle that caught her around the waist. The force of Robert's forward momentum sent them both falling backward onto his bed, but Serena was fighting mad, and she came up kicking.

"How could you treat me like that? Just pick me up and carry me off like a sack of potatoes? I've never been so embarrassed in my entire life!" she raged, arms and legs flailing.

"Ouch!" Robert grunted as one of her shoes connected with his shin. "I'm warning you, Serena, knock it off, or I'm really going to lose my temper."

Since his threat fell on deaf ears, Robert had to employ action, and in a matter of seconds Serena was lying under him, limp and out of breath. Taking advantage of her lack of strength, Robert stared down into her flushed face and admonished, "I don't want to hurt you, but you're going to stay put until we get to the bottom of this adolescent behavior. Steven could see that you're young, but did you have to go out of your way to convince him that I'm robbing the cradle?"

"Your brother's not worried about the difference in our ages," Serena cried. "He's concerned about the difference in our backgrounds. I warned you that people were going to feel this way about me, Robert, but you refused to believe it. I admit that I didn't try very hard to get him to like me, but it wouldn't have made any difference to him if I had. He made up his mind about me before we met, and he's not going to change it."

Robert moved off her, but kept a firm grip on her wrists. "That's ridiculous!" he exclaimed. "Steven's not like that at all."

"The heck he isn't," Serena retorted, struggling to sit up, and irked that she couldn't manage the feat until Robert allowed it. "You saw his face when I walked in tonight. He took one look at me and practically had a stroke."

To Serena's vexation, Robert had the nerve to laugh. "He was shocked all right," he admitted. "But then, how was he supposed to guess that there was a normal woman beneath this getup?"

"If you'd wanted him to know about me, you would have told him," Serena charged, unable to keep the hurt out of her voice. "But you knew exactly how he'd react if he found out who I really am. That's why you told me to behave myself around him. You were hoping he'd leave here without ever knowing that you've gotten yourself involved with a beggarly gypsy."

Shaking his head incredulously, Robert sighed. "I knew I handled this badly, but believe me, Serena, I never meant to hurt you. I was trying to keep you from being hurt."

"Because you knew that your brother would never accept me," Serena insisted.

"Maybe you'll understand this better if I explain something that's different between my world and yours."

"So you *do* understand that there are differences," Serena came back, feeling no triumph at his admittance. "Huge, insurmountable differences."

Ignoring her last comment as if she hadn't spoken, Robert continued, "Remember how you told me that your grandmother was in charge of finding you a husband, and how you felt she had the right since she was the most senior member of your family?"

"Of course I remember."

"Well, Steven is the eldest member of my family, but, as far as I'm concerned, when it comes to what I decide to do, that seniority doesn't give him any rights at all," Robert said. "I'm a grown man, and I don't need or want his opinion, especially when it comes to the woman in my life. Unfortunately, that doesn't prevent him from offering it."

"You say that, Robert, but I think you care very much what Steven thinks. You want his approval just as much as I wanted my grandmother's."

"Because I love and respect him, just like you loved and respected her," Robert retorted. "But there's a difference, Serena. You never thought of going against your grandmother's wishes, but I go up against Steven's all the time. I choose my own women, and I run my own life.''

"Then if Steven's opinion about me doesn't matter to you, why were you so nervous about him meeting me?'' Serena wanted to know.

"Because the woman I love is young and sweet, but she's not sure she can trust in her feelings for me, and she's still uncertain about our future. I knew Steven was going to start prying, and I didn't want him stumbling into any sensitive areas.''

"I'm very certain that I love you, Robert, but you're right about the future," Serena burst out vehemently. "When it comes to forever, there's far more to consider than our love for one another, and whatever you say, family is very important to you.''

"*You're* what's important to me,'' Robert replied, "even when you get all defensive for no reason and go off half-cocked like you did tonight.''

Serena considered his words for several moments. "I suppose I am overly sensitive about certain things,'' she said softly.

Robert reached out with one finger and wiped away a streak of black liner that had smudged under her eye. "You only suppose?''

"Okay, I am.''

"If you'd given Steven half a chance, you would've found out that he doesn't judge people by their pedigrees. Once he saw through your act, he was ready to start liking you. He admires guts, and any woman who would show up looking like you did tonight has to have more than her share.''

When Robert leaned over to kiss her and his mouth came away stained in red, Serena had to laugh. ''Maybe I did go a tad overboard on the makeup.''

''Maybe just a tad,'' Robert agreed, wiping his mouth on his sleeve. ''Are there really that many people who give you a hard time without even knowing you?''

''Grannie and I were run out of so many places, I've lost count,'' Serena admitted. ''When people find out there are gypsies in town, they assume they're going to steal things from them or curse them with bad luck or make off with their children.''

''Do people still believe in those old wive's tales?''

''So much so that I'm afraid I've come to expect that kind of prejudice in everybody,'' Serena conceded. ''Outrunning people's suspicions has become a way of life to me.''

Robert's expression became thoughtful. ''You didn't run this time, Serena.''

''No,'' Serena said. ''This time I was determined to give as good as I got.''

''Because you love me,'' Robert concluded with a smug smile.

''Because I love you,'' Serena agreed.

Rolling her beneath him, Robert murmured, ''One day at a time, painted lady. Together, we can conquer your fear of forever if we just keep taking it one day at a time.''

Serena's lips parted to accept his kiss, but then she caught sight of something out of the corner of her eye. "Robert, someone just slipped a piece of paper under your door."

Nuzzling her neck, Robert mumbled, "Uh-huh."

"Aren't you going to get up and see what it is?"

"It's probably a farewell note from my brother."

"You think he's leaving!" Serena cried.

Robert didn't seem to be the least bit troubled by that possibility. "He got what he came for."

"But Robert!" Serena turned her head to escape his questing mouth. "We can't let him leave now. After the way I behaved tonight, what must he think?"

"He thinks we make a perfect couple," Robert assured her, then captured her lips to forestall any other needless questions.

Nine

In 1823 the Ladies Aid Society of the village of Tewksberry had sponsored a Rural Ball to be held on the Ides of March in the Old Liberty Pavilion. The founders of the society, Theodora Tewksberry and Rose Armstrong had conceived of the idea to raise funds in charitable support of the Tewksberry Foundling Home. The orphanage had closed its doors soon after World War I, but the Rural Ball was still held right on schedule every year and the proceeds divided between several public organizations.

Although the original purpose for the affair no longer existed, some things hadn't changed from its beginning. The Rural Ball was still considered the social event of the season, and attendance was required of all but the most undesirable element. Since the

Armstrong family had been represented at the ball for
over one hundred and fifty years, the new owner of
Laurel Glen had received one of the first invitations.

It took some persuasion, but eventually Robert
managed to convince Serena that they should attend
the affair together. Resigned to the knowledge that as
Robert's date she was going to be subject to the intense scrutiny of Tewksberry's most prominent and
influential citizens, Serena dressed very carefully for
the evening. Any woman would be proud to be seen
with Robert, but Serena wanted the opposite to be
true, as well.

Reminding herself that adaptation was not assimi-
lation, she'd purchased a pale peach silk dress, knowing it would be far more appropriate for the occasion
than anything else she owned. For Robert's sake, she
wasn't out looking for trouble. Instead, she intended
to do her best to fit in. The dress she chose was exotic
but not overly so as it fell from one shoulder leaving
the other bare, tastefully taking advantage of the
draping qualities of the fabric.

As expected, Robert wore a conservative black tux-
edo, and he carried the formal attire as naturally as he
did a sweater and jeans. Unlike Serena, who was worried that she wouldn't be able to keep up her ladylike
demeanor for an entire night, Robert exuded the
masculine grace and assurance so apparent in those
who were born to the manor. Even though Serena
didn't possess Robert's innate confidence, as soon as
they stepped into the pavilion, they were both greeted

as charter members of an elite society that could be traced back as far as the Mayflower.

In keeping with tradition, the huge ballroom was lit only by candles, and the walls were draped with the fragrant boughs of balsam fir. In the banquet hall, members of the founding families were seated at the head table, and the rest of the company were placed in subsequent rows according to social position, the least noteworthy occupying tables closest to the kitchen. After an excellent dinner provided by the Merchant Association, the guests were invited to dance to the music of the Singing Strings Orchestra, a group made up of retired local musicians.

Refreshments for the evening were served by volunteers from the Ladies Aid. Members of the society were schooled not to comment on the amount of any donation placed in the large basket at the center of their table, but Serena noticed quite a few raised eyebrows as Robert stopped by to deposit his check.

As he recaptured Serena's hand and guided her back onto the dance floor, they overheard several comments from the refreshment committee.

"He's an Armstrong to be sure," one woman observed. "And most generous. I'm so glad that he came to represent the family."

"He's a fine addition to the community," agreed another. "And I do hope that wedding bells are in the offing. She's British, you know."

"They *do* make a perfectly lovely couple, don't they?" gushed a third.

"What did I tell you?" Robert whispered in Serena's ear as he took her into his arms. "Even Tewksberry's oldest and finest think we're a great match."

"Money talks," Serena whispered back.

"But now with your delightfully British accent," Robert retorted. "I'm almost positive that they switched our place cards up to the head table when you entered on my arm."

"Not very likely, oh revered one," Serena came back, laughing as Robert punished her irreverence by whirling her around and around and around.

No matter what Robert said, Serena didn't think the local matrons would be so enamored with her once they learned the truth about her background. But she discovered she was wrong. As she stood in the powder room, she was approached by a robust white-haired woman who introduced herself as Claudia Tewksberry, her hostess for the evening and the current president of the Ladies Aid.

"Oh, my dear," the woman exclaimed breathlessly, "I'm so glad I have this chance to speak with you. It's my lumbago, you see. It acts up every winter, but this year, it's gotten so much worse."

Not sure how to respond to this information, Serena inquired tentatively, "Your lumbago?"

"Oh my, yes. Just ask my dear friend Rebecca," Claudia gestured to another older woman who was standing nearby, readjusting the combs in her lacquered silver hair. "She can tell you how I suffer."

With a pleasant smile, the woman stepped forward to offer Serena her hand. "I'm Rebecca Preston, and, as the mayor's wife, Claudia and I sit on several committees together. Eugenia Riley has told us how your herbal remedies have helped her arthritis, and we simply couldn't wait to meet you. I was hoping that you could recommend something to improve my general vitality."

Claudia concurred with her friend's statement. "I've always believed that it's best to try to regain one's health naturally. After all, we are part of a continuum of being, and therefore our condition must be linked to the influences of natural organic substances. Unfortunately, in the name of scientific progress, we've foolishly discarded the baby with the bathwater. I say, if the old ways work best, why not stick to them?"

Rebecca smiled. "At my age, it does my heart good to find someone who believes that our outdated thinking has some merit after all. I've tried to convince my grandchildren that pills aren't a cure-all for everything, but to no avail. I know that some of my mother's home remedies work just as well as the artificially processed cures one can buy over the counter today, but they refuse to believe it."

Serena was in for another surprise when Claudia took up the idea again. Even if she tried she wouldn't have been able to respond to either woman's comments. "Thank heavens there are still some people left with the wisdom to retain so much of the old knowledge and pass it on to the next generation. Mark my words, one of these days we'll have to acknowledge a huge debt of thanks to you gypsies and our Native Americans for preserving a science that should never have been allowed to die out."

It was a full twenty minutes before Serena walked out into the hall where Robert was talking with several other men. Upon seeing her he immediately excused himself and came to her side. "I was beginning to think you'd been shanghaied in there," he complained.

"I was, and it's a lucky thing for you that this happened," Serena replied happily, a bemused expression on her face. "A lucky thing for both of us."

"That what happened?"

Still smiling, Serena took Robert's arm. "I'll be happy to tell you, but let's go outside on the terrace to talk. I know it's cold out there, but it's a beautiful clear night, and I want to see the stars."

"Sure," Robert said, enthralled by the joyful air about her and anxious to know what was behind it. Whatever the cause, he was grateful. Ever since Serena had learned that she wasn't pregnant, there'd been a sadness in her eyes, but for the past several days Robert had feared that there was a direct correlation between her growing depression and the fast-approaching deadline for her departure. All along, his biggest worry had been that his attempt to hold on to her would diminish that radiant inner glow that made her such a unique and special person, and recently it had seemed to him as if that fear was coming true.

Robert loved her more than his own life, but if his love diminished her in any way, he knew that when the time came he would have to find the strength to let her go. Now there was a chance he wouldn't have to. At least, that was the feeling he was getting as Serena led him outside.

"So what went on in there?" he demanded as soon as they were through the double French doors.

Happy to tell him, Serena relayed the conversation she'd just had with two of the town's leading matriarchs. She went on to say that their enthusiastic interest in her profession wasn't nearly as important as the effect the incident had had on her unsettled state of mind. "I've learned so much since coming to Laurel Glen, but one of the most surprising things I've discovered is that prejudice works both ways."

Gazing up at the stars, she continued, "From the time I was born, I was taught that the *gaje* would always view me as an outcast. Grannie drummed that belief into my head so thoroughly that I stopped questioning whether or not it was true in all cases. When I met you, I sincerely believed that you were the one and only exception to this rule, but that made perfect sense to me since you were the man Grannie had seen in her vision."

Serena stopped talking when she glanced over at Robert in time to catch him rolling his eyes heavenward. "Okay, I know how you feel about that, but I'm trying to explain my motivations."

"Go right ahead," Robert encouraged, promising not to interrupt her again.

Wrinkling her nose at his insincere tone, Serena went on. "I was always expecting rejection, and so I found it, even when it wasn't really there. If you'll recall, I made a complete fool out of myself when I met your brother."

"How could I forget? And I'm sure Steven won't," Robert said with a grin.

Serena grimaced. "Yet, according to the letter you got from him afterward, he understood and didn't hold it against me."

"Steven's a pretty understanding guy."

"Which makes two people who don't judge others by outside appearance," Serena said. "And Conlan makes three, and then there's Betty and Harold and Mrs. Riley and Bill Murdock and—"

"And the list goes on and on," Robert continued.

"Exactly," Serena said. "But up until tonight, I never would have believed that those high-society types I met in the ladies' room could be added to that number. And if those two pillars of the community view life with an open mind, why should I assume that all those other people I was so worried about won't feel the same way?"

Robert frowned. "All what other people?"

"Your business associates and friends, all the important people you have to cultivate in order to reestablish Laurel Glen."

Robert shook his finger at her. "How many times do I have to tell you that those supposedly important other people don't matter to me? *You're* the only one who matters, Serena."

"Well, that mattered to me," Serena retorted. "I could never have been happy if I thought I stood in the way of your dreams."

Robert's ears perked up at her use of the past tense. "Meaning you're no longer worried about doing that?"

"No, I'm not," Serena confirmed. "I'm sure we'll run into some who will look down their noses at me, but that's their problem, not mine."

"Please remind me to increase my donation to the Ladies Aid for the great service they've performed to-night on my behalf," Robert exclaimed exuberantly, pulling Serena into his arms and kissing her soundly. "And the next time I run into Claudia Tewksberry, she's going to get the same treatment."

"She'll be so thrilled," Serena giggled as she snuggled deeper into his embrace. "We can work this thing out, Robert. I just know we can. If you're willing to make a few compromises, there's nothing to keep us apart."

"If being together is the end result, I'm willing to do almost anything, but what about you?" Robert inquired, his eyes narrowed on her face. "Are you sure this is what you want?"

"More than I can say," Serena admitted. "I just didn't think it could be possible."

"And what about your itchy feet?" Robert asked. "Have you worked out that problem, too?"

"I've come to love Laurel Glen, Robert," Serena said. "And I want to raise our children there, but there's no rule that says we can't travel."

"No, there isn't."

"And you'll come with me?"

"Absolutely."

"Then, as far as I'm concerned, we can forget all about that silly deadline. I've already made my decision."

"Hallelujah!" Robert sighed in relief. "Waiting for you to make up your mind has been driving me out of mine."

"I love you, Robert," Serena murmured, pulling his head down so she could kiss him. "And we're going to be so happy together."

"That we will, sweetheart," Robert agreed wholeheartedly as he brought his lips down to hers.

As always, Serena reveled in the joy of being loved and wanted by him, and without hesitation she proved that those feelings were mutual. She kissed him with open hunger, the glow inside her warming them both until the heat was so intense that they either had to break apart or cause a scandal that would rock the hallowed halls of the Old Liberty Pavilion for years to come.

"I thought you said it was going to be cold out here," Robert teased, taking a deep breath as he set her away from him. "It seems plenty hot to me. So hot that I think we'd better go home and get out of all these uncomfortable clothes."

"You won't hear any arguments from me," Serena murmured breathlessly, gazing up at him with adoring eyes. "But what are people going to think about us if we leave early?"

Half amused, half exasperated, Robert challenged, "Do we care what other people think about us?"

"Not in the least," Serena tossed off airily, and tucked her arm through his. "If anyone asks, we'll just tell them that we were called home because something urgent has come up."

"I'll say it has," Robert confirmed, his downward glance making his meaning so obvious that Serena blushed. "Maybe we should sneak around the back way and disappear into the night before anyone else notices."

With a mischievous gleam in her eye, Serena tugged on his arm. "But we don't care what people think. Remember?"

Robert allowed himself to be pulled closer to the door. "I know at least what the men will be thinking if they notice the look in my eyes. They'll decide it's time to get their wives home and in bed, and couples will start leaving in droves."

Serena hesitated, then stopped. "Well, we certainly can't be responsible for a mass desertion. The Ladies Aid would never forgive us."

"Like I said, we should sneak out before anyone notices that we're gone."

Trying to sound like a model of decorum, Serena conceded solemnly, "Upon further consideration, I think that would indeed be best."

Robert captured her hand, and, like two errant children, they started running along the narrow balustrade that surrounded the outside of the building. Once they'd reached the front, Robert slipped through the door and retrieved their coats, and a few minutes later they were inside the car and racing back to Laurel Glen.

The next morning Robert opened his eyes to find Serena perched on the edge of the bed, her gaze fixed lovingly on him. He blinked up at her, then smiled blissfully. His body felt heavy and sated, soothed by the marvelous lassitude that comes with total fulfillment. "It's too early," he grumbled as his eyes drifted closed again. "Get back under the covers, and let's snuggle for another couple of hours."

"Okay," Serena replied agreeably, sliding down beneath the quilts until her naked body was curled up comfortably next to his. "But you'll have to get used to getting up this early when we're on the road."

It took several moments for her words to register, and once they did, Robert still didn't have any idea what she was talking about. "Huh?"

Sitting up again, Serena pointed to the window she had pushed open earlier. "Just breath that air, Robert. Can't you smell the new life in it? The promise of springtime?"

Robert sniffed and shrugged. "I can't smell much of anything."

"Trust me," Serena said. "Winter is on its way out, and it won't be coming back. We gypsies have a second sense about such things, but if you don't believe me, go find yourself a woolly worm. Their cocoons are so thin that it's a sure bet spring will come early this year."

Still not following, Robert sat up beside her, shivering as a draft of cold air blew in from the open window. Grabbing for the quilt he said, "I think you're trying to tell me something here, but so far all I'm catching from this conversation is a cold."

Unlike him, Serena seemed to be invigorated by the stiff breeze, and she held out her arms as if to embrace the cool air. "You'll get used to it," she promised. "By this time next week, I bet we'll be sleeping with the door open."

"What door?"

"The door to our caravan."

Robert repeated her words dumbly and Serena nodded. "Especially if we head south. We'll need to take enough time for you to learn whether you can do this every year, but luckily we won't have to travel very far to find our first fair. I happen to know that there's one thing held in the Poconos next weekend."

"In the Poconos," Robert recited inanely. "Next weekend."

"The Newcastle Colonial Craft Fair," Serena informed him. "I thought I was going to miss it since I wouldn't be leaving here until April, but now I won't have to. And if it's as well attended as it was three years ago, we stand to make a good profit."

Noting Robert's blank expression, Serena grinned. "The tourists stand in line to buy my spice balls and sachets, especially the ones I make out of lavender. All those old Colonial ladies used to reek of lavender."

It was beginning to dawn on Robert that Serena wasn't joking. "You don't really expect me to travel by wagon to Pennsylvania, and help you sell spice balls at some rinky-dink fair?''

"I'll have you know that I do some of my best business at rinky-dink fairs,'' Serena retorted indignantly.

"You're serious about this!'' Robert exclaimed.

"Of course, I'm serious,'' Serena replied. "How else are we going to find out if you can handle life on the road if you don't experience it?''

Thinking back to last night's conversation, Robert realized what she'd meant by compromise. "This is the kind of travel you were talking about? You want us to roam around the country, selling herbal concoctions out of that rickety old wagon of yours?''

"That's what travel means to a gyspy, Robert,'' Serena stated quietly. "And selling herbal concoctions is what a Drabarnie does. In case you've forgotten, that's what I am.''

Something in her tone caught Robert's attention. As he looked down into her face, it was as if he were watching a radiant light that was starting to dim. All at once he understood that the way he handled the next few minutes would determine whether or not that light went out completely, and he quickly lost his resistance to her outlandish idea. Last night he'd told her that he was game for anything if it meant they could be together, and Robert prided himself on being a man of his word. "When would we have to leave?''

"I'd like to go this afternoon.''

Robert's mind immediately filled with a hundred reasons why he couldn't possibly get ready for such a trip in so short a time, but since he could see by her expression that Serena was expecting him to voice every one of them, he didn't. "How long do you expect us to be gone?"

"At least two weeks."

"Two weeks." Robert considered her words.

"Maybe longer."

"How much longer?"

Serena threw up her hands in frustration. "I don't know, and I won't know until I'm out on the road."

Taking a deep breath, she elaborated, "I can't explain it, but something happens to me every spring. I smell all that new life in the air, and the vagabond spirit rises up in me so strong that I can't resist it. All I know is that I have to be totally free to go wherever the spirit takes me."

"Every spring, huh?" Robert contemplated the prospect of throwing off all the restraints imposed on him by modern society and taking off for parts unknown for several weeks out of every year. To his surprise the idea didn't seem nearly so off-the-wall to him as it had only a few moments before. There just might be something to be said for Serena's Bohemian philosophy, even though he couldn't imagine himself embracing it to the extent she did. Yet, didn't every man deserve some time off from the toils and cares of life?

"Each and every spring," Serena reiterated, just to make sure that Robert completely understood what he was letting himself in for. "I don't expect you to give up your life-style for me, but I want you to understand why I can't completely give up mine. I'm hoping that this trip will accomplish what I can't put into words."

"In that case," he said, "what the devil are we doing lazing around in this bed?"

Not waiting to see her reaction, Robert rolled swiftly off the mattress and strode into the bathroom. When he returned from his shower ten minutes later, Serena was still sitting in the same position, staring solemnly off into space. She didn't even notice that he was back until he exclaimed, "C'mon, lazybones. Get out of that bed. If we don't want to miss out on the fair, we've got to get this show on the road."

"Robert?"

"Hmm?"

"I'm not forcing you to come with me," Serena said. "If you really can't get away on such short notice, I'll understand."

Robert shook his head at her as he pulled on his jeans. "A deal's a deal, Serena."

"But you didn't understand what I was talking about when you agreed to it," Serena said. "So it isn't fair for me to expect you to accept my terms."

"You make it sound as if you're asking me to jump off the Brooklyn Bridge or something," Robert teased. "I think you've forgotten that I was a cowboy long before I became a gentleman farmer. I'm used to roughing it."

"Living like a gypsy on the road isn't the same as camping out on the open range for a couple of days."

Robert chuckled at her concern. "I think I can manage to deal with a few hardships."

"It's not the hardships that concern me," Serena came back. "I don't think you realize what kind of cooperation it takes to live in such close quarters day after day."

"As long as it's with you, I'll be just fine."

Although Serena knew he felt that way now, she wasn't so certain he would feel that way in the future. But then, that was the purpose of this trip, wasn't it? "I know I'm asking a lot of you, but I'm prepared to give a lot in return."

Robert heard the quiver in her voice and decided that all the work he would be forced to leave undone, all the plans that had to be put on hold and the business meetings that would have to be postponed to a later date didn't matter to him at all. Nothing mattered but Serena's happiness. With a lascivious grin on his face, he replied, "And I'm prepared to take it." Then he scooped her up out of bed and carried her into the bathroom.

Robert received a passionate kiss each step he took along the way. By the time he set her down inside the shower enclosure, he wasn't adverse to the idea of joining her. Sliding his hands down her naked back, he explored the hollows of her spine. She was so delicately made, yet she had the power to control him with a wave of her hand.

"If you need help washing your back, I'm your man," he offered hoarsely, his eyes caressing the lovely curves of her breasts and hips as she stepped under the warm spray.

With an impish smile, Serena closed the shower door in his face. "I appreciate the magnanimous offer, but if I accepted, we might not get out of here until tomorrow."

Even if they never stepped a foot off Laurel Glen for the rest of their lives, Robert knew that there would still be times when he would neglect his schedule in order to spend more time with her. So, in the long run, what difference would it make if they stayed close to home all the time or roamed around the countryside? He firmly believed that when a man got married he had to change his priorities.

It just so happened that *this* man was going to marry a gypsy, and she required much more freedom than the average woman.

Ten

"What are you doing?" Serena demanded as she watched Robert lift the heavy kerosene heater out of the back of her caravan. "I know I said it was going to get warm soon, but we still might need that some night."

Paying no attention to her, Robert walked into the stable. A few minutes later he and Bill Murdock returned, carrying a large cardboard box. "If you've got any other packing to do, you might as well do it now," Robert said, ducking back inside the stable door to retrieve more boxes. "It'll take us a while to install this portable generator and another hour or so to hook up the heater and wire the lights."

Serena was incredulous. "When did you decide to do all this?"

"As soon as I found out you were riding around in a firetrap," Robert replied. "I was going to surprise you with it if you decided to leave without me, but I thought I had more time to get everything ready."

Serena didn't quite know how she felt about the modernization of her caravan. It was very generous of Robert to buy her all this new equipment, and she had to admit that electricity was far safer than kerosene, but she'd never had a single fire in all the years she'd been traveling. Somehow, electrical lights didn't seem half as romantic as the soft glow from an oil lamp, and there was something odd about heating a horse-drawn trailer with an electrical appliance.

Even so, Robert looked so pleased with himself that she found herself thanking him. However, when she came back outside at noon and saw him trying to find room inside the caravan for a butane cookstove, a battery-operated radio and a portable toilet, she had to draw the line. "I'm sorry, Robert, but the object of this trip is to escape the trappings of civilization. How can we do that if you plan to take it all with us?"

"Is there something in the gypsy handbook that says we have to do everything the hard way?" Robert said, surprised by the accusation.

"Not the hard way," Serena retorted. "The old way, the traditional way. You understand the importance of tradition, don't you, Robert?"

"But in this day and age, it's just plain silly to totally rough it," he complained. "What if we run into bad weather? How will we know how serious it is if we don't bring a radio?"

"That's part of the challenge of living close to nature," she informed him.

Reluctantly Robert reached for the radio. "Okay, this can go, but I still think we should keep the stove. What if we can't find any dry wood to start a fire? We'll be stuck eating cold food."

"Heat doesn't alter the nutritional value, and it won't kill us to eat a few cold meals."

Serena had yet to come right out and call him a sissy, but the implication was there in her tone, so Robert didn't put up further arguments. "Do you have anything against flashlights?" he inquired testily, as he removed the cookstove and toilet.

Annoyed by his attitude, Serena turned on her heel and walked into the stable. "If you feel you must have a flashlight, then by all means bring one."

Robert was still glaring at the doorway when she came back out leading William. She shot him a saccharine-sweet smile. "Unless you need more than what you've got packed in those two big duffel bags, we can head out as soon as I hitch up the horse."

"By that, are you trying to tell me that my stuff takes up too much room?"

Serena shrugged. "I plan to wash clothes along the way, but if you'd rather bring your entire wardrobe, feel free."

"I'm not bringing my entire wardrobe!" Robert shouted. "I know you think we're in for some kind of a heat wave, but just in case you and your woolly worms are wrong, I packed some warm clothes."

"Fine," Serena snapped, insulted by his lack faith in her weather prediction. "But you're not going to need them."

"We'll see," Robert retorted spitefully, then told her he would be ready to leave as soon as he double-checked to make sure that Mrs. Riley had everything she needed to keep the household running smoothly until their return. Since the woman had never required Robert's input in that area before, Serena assumed he wanted some time to cool off. He had to be as much aware as she was that in a short while they were going to be stuck together in very cramped quarters, and, no matter how angry they became with each other, they were going to have to tough it out.

Thinking about the strong possibility that she and Robert weren't going to make good traveling companions, Serena was no longer as eager to make the trip as she had been a few hours ago. When she'd relayed her grand plan to Robert early this morning, she'd suspected that he wasn't that enamored with the idea, but then he'd done a complete about-face and convinced her that he was sincerely looking forward to the trip. She could see now, however, that his enthusiasm was phony. Whatever he thought, he wouldn't be able to keep up his act for any great lengths of time.

Last night she'd assumed that they'd finally found a workable solution to their problems, but now she wasn't so sure. Unfortunately, it was beginning to look as though her satisfaction with the arrangement was premature for Robert's idea of travel included all the modern conveniences of home.

In her naive fantasy, Serena had pictured them roaming the countryside together, picking wildflowers in the grassy meadows, cooking their meals over an open camp fire and dancing beneath the stars. She'd imagined them having a fantastic time, but if Robert adopted the kind of attitude he'd displayed this morning, she would be taking her future trips alone. Knowing Robert, he wouldn't be able to tolerate a wife who took off on her own whenever the spirit moved her, and that would put them right back at square one. They loved each other, but a marriage between them would never work.

Serena was extremely depressed by the time she drove the wagon up the driveway to the main house. It was forty-five minutes later, but there was still no sign of Robert. Obviously he wasn't in any great hurry to get started, or it wouldn't be taking him this long to conduct his last-minute conversation with Mrs. Riley. Or maybe he was using these delaying tactics to work up his courage so he could tell Serena he'd changed his mind about going. If she was having second thoughts about the wisdom of this trip, it was logical to think that he might be, too.

Expecting the worse, Serena was astounded when Robert came bounding down the wide white marble steps as soon as she pulled up at the front portico. All Serena could do was gape at him, for he was wearing hand-tooled leather boots, tight black pants with a red sash around his waist and an embroidered Western vest over a white shirt with long flowing sleeves. The crowning touch was the red bandanna he wore on his head.

Laughing at her stunned expression, Robert climbed up onto the wagon seat. "When in Rome, it's polite to do what the Romans do," he informed her with a dimpled smile.

Not for the world was Serena going to tell him that he looked more like a cross between a pirate and a cowboy than a gypsy. He'd obviously gone to such great pains to make himself into the traveling companion he thought she wanted and Serena felt as if her heart were going to burst. Was it any wonder she adored this man?

"You cut a very dashing figure, me boyo," she complimented, all the love she felt for him shining in her eyes. "Once they catch sight of you, our female customers will rush over to lay down their money."

"And when their husbands spy you, we'll double our profits," Robert assured her, beaming with pleasure when Serena offered him William's reins.

"The honor of driving always goes to the strongest member of the *kumpania*."

"*Kumpania?*" Robert inquired as he accepted the reins.

"Our traveling band," Serena explained, then added, "Even a band as small as ours must have a strong leader to hold us together when we face the adventures and hardships that await us."

"A leader is only as strong as his followers," Robert declared wisely. "Which makes me a very lucky man."

"Thank you, kind sir," Serena replied demurely.

"Shall we be off then, my beauty?"

"We shall," Serena agreed happily. As they passed through the gates of Laurel Glen, she began to sing an old childhood song.

We must be off on the roads again,
for the call has come to roam,
that wild call, that clear call
to wander far from home.

We must be off on the roads again,
to the vagrant gypsy life,
And all we ask is a clear blue sky
and winds like a whetted knife.

When Serena had spoken of hardships, Robert had thought she was referring to camping outdoors in miserable weather and eating cold food. He hadn't considered the possibility of being half-drowned while fording a swollen stream or being shot at by some lunatic farmer who didn't want trespassers on his land. He hadn't comprehended the hazards of driving a wagon on the side of a highway with cars whizzing by right and left, or being stopped by a patrol car and told to move on or risk being arrested for vagrancy. Adding insult to injury, while he vacillated between fear for his life and frustration, Serena appeared to take all of these unnerving incidents in stride.

By the time they reached the Pocono Mountains and made camp on the outskirts of the village of Newcastle, Robert felt dirty and exhausted and thoroughly irritated by Serena's unflagging high spirits. And it didn't help matters any to acknowledge that they hadn't made love since leaving Laurel Glen because he just didn't have enough energy by the end of the day.

"I don't know what you're so all-fired happy about," Robert declared testily as he hauled his stiff body down from the wagon seat and observed Serena's delight over the nearness of a half-frozen lake. "As far as I'm concerned, the three hours it took us to find this out-of-the-way place could have been much better spent."

Undaunted by his disagreeable tone, Serena sighed happily, "But isn't it lovely?"

"It's a pretty spot," Robert agreed with an uncaring shrug.

"This is the same special place where Grannie and I camped three years ago. I was so afraid I wouldn't be able to find it again."

Robert surveyed the surrounding area, but couldn't see anything that made this small clearing stand out from any of the other ones where they'd stopped. Admittedly, with the rolling hills, luxuriant forest and the colorful rock cliffs around them, it was a beautiful setting, but Serena had a knack for finding beautiful settings, and, in the past few days he'd learned that the owner of such scenic locations was usually the state.

"I assume this is another game preserve or a bird sanctuary or something, and we're parked unlawfully again," he grumbled. "What kind of fine will we be expected to pay if we get caught this time?"

Serena tossed off his concern, her expression showing how trivial she thought the problem. "If we don't get caught, we won't have to pay anything."

"Right," Robert said, startled when he caught sight of another trailer parked between two tall evergreens some distance away.

"Look over there," he directed Serena. "We've got company."

"With the Newcastle fair starting tomorrow, we'll probably have lots more before nightfall," Serena replied.

"Why would you think that?"

"Because this is one of the safe stops on the Rom network."

Robert was fast on her heels as Serena climbed up into the caravan and began changing out of her clothes. Before he could question her on her reason for disrobing, he wanted to get to the bottom of this Rom network thing. "What network?"

As if she were revealing secret knowledge that might jeopardize national security, Serena told him that the gypsies had a system of favored routes that led from the deep South all the way up into Canada. Here and there along each route were isolated campsites that were designated as safe stops. Away from the disapproving eyes of local authorities, these sites were uninhabited by the *gaje* and generally unknown to anyone but those who were privy to the unwritten gypsy code.

"With any luck," she concluded, "we'll run into some of Grannie's old friends who've come for the fair. It was always assumed that I'd never find a man, so I can't wait to show you off."

Suddenly Robert got the uncomfortable feeling that he'd been hoodwinked into attending some weird kind of ragtag reunion. "I thought you said that you and your grandmother weren't accepted by the Rom."

Stripped down to her underwear, Serena reached up to open the cupboard over her cot. "Our blood would never be allowed to mix with theirs, but that didn't prohibit us from forming friendships with other gypsy travelers. They'll be happy to have us join in their party tonight, especially since this is a safe stop. If this was a formal gathering of the Rom, then we'd definitely be excluded, but everyone is welcome here."

With an impish smile she added, "Even a *gaje* man like you, if he's been approved by one of us."

"Did you know about this gathering before we left Laurel Glen?"

"I knew that other gypsies would be attending the fair and would probably camp here for the night," Serena admitted. "But I don't have any idea if I'll know any of them," she quickly added when she saw his thunderous scowl.

As Robert digested this sudden turn of events Serena tossed him a towel, hoping he would be in a better mood once they'd cleaned themselves up. "C'mon. If we're going to a party tonight, we need to take a bath."

Robert narrowed his brows suspiciously as she wrapped herself in a blanket and turned toward the door. "C'mon where?"

"There's a big tub of clean water waiting for us right out there."

"You want me to jump into that frozen lake of my own free will?"

Serena giggled and challenged, "I'll give you time to get down to your shorts, but after that, the last one in is a rotten egg."

Robert felt the gooseflesh rise up on his body just thinking about it. "How about we heat a kettle of water over the fire and make do with a sponge bath."

Serena shook her head. "Look at us, Robert. We're both a mess. A sponge bath won't do the job. Of course, if you're afraid of a little cold water..." Her voice trailed off mockingly.

As childish as it was, Robert rose to the challenge and began stripping off his clothes. "Okay, you're on, lady, but this is the last time you put down my masculinity and get away with it."

Serena looked surprised. "When have I ever put down your masculinity?"

"I don't know what else you'd call it," Robert growled. "Just because I don't like being shot at or run out of town by the police doesn't make me a wimp."

Horrified that he'd jumped to such an erroneous conclusion, Serena exclaimed, "I don't think that. Considering that you've never had those kinds of things happen to you before, I think you've been an awfully good sport. Other than being a bit on the surly side occasionally, you haven't made a single complaint this whole trip. I'm sure any wimp worth his salt would've started bellyaching as soon as we got stuck in a ditch, but you didn't."

Somewhat mollified but still not completely convinced of her sincerity, Robert reminded her, "No, but I almost broke my toe when I kicked that stupid tire."

"Well, I almost broke mine kicking the other one."

"You did!"

"Of course I did," Serena said. "But it's not fair to take out your frustrations on your traveling companion. After all, it wasn't your fault that the road was that muddy and I fell flat on my face in the muck."

For the first time in a hundred miles, Robert's dimples came out in full force. "This might not be very nice of me, but I considered that one of the highlights of this trip. With all that dirt on your face, I got a well-deserved break from that cheery smile you've been wearing from dawn to dusk every day."

Serena sniffed indignantly. "I was just trying to look on the bright side of things. So far this trip hasn't exactly been a barrel of laughs, but I was hoping, if I kept on smiling, you might not notice what a rotten time we were having."

Their eyes met over that ridiculous statement, and they both burst out laughing at the same time. A second later they were in each other's arms. "Oh, Robert," Serena sighed. "It wasn't supposed to be like this."

"I know, sweetheart," Robert assured her tenderly. "But now that we're back on the same side, it can only get better."

Serena hugged him tightly, so relieved that they were communicating again that she wanted to cry. "If you'd rather find a more private place to camp, it's fine with me. The only person I need to be with right now is you."

"And miss out on a great party?" Robert smiled down into her face as he set her away from him. "I think two people who've been through what we have this week deserve some kind of a celebration, don't you?"

"Do you mean it, Robert?" Serena asked. "You really wouldn't mind if we stayed?"

"I'm looking forward to it," Robert replied, and Serena knew that this time he wasn't just trying to appease her.

"You won't be sorry," Serena promised as she went up on tiptoe to kiss him. "Tonight will be a night to remember."

Four hours later, as he stood outside a circle of a dozen blazing camp fires, Robert knew that he would remember this night forever. Just as Serena had predicted, by the time the sun had gone down, a number of other wagons had joined theirs in the clearing. Although it turned out that she didn't know any of the twenty-or-so other people who'd arrived, both she and Robert were accepted as fellow travelers and were welcome to join in the festivities.

At first Robert was subject to a variety of stares, some wary, others merely curious. Luckily he'd noticed how the other men were dressed before he'd ventured outside in his idea of a gypsy costume. Very kindly, Serena hadn't told him that his outfit would be more appropriate for a Halloween party than it was for an actual gathering of the Rom.

Although one or two of the men wore an earring, none of them had bandannas on their heads or colorful sashes around their waists. They wore clothing suitable for the weather. Since it was a pleasantly warm spring night, that meant long-sleeved shirts or sweaters, and jeans. Not wanting to feel more out of place than he already did, Robert did likewise.

The women, on the other hand, wore outfits that better fit the stereotype. Later Robert was to learn that gypsy men had allowed themselves to progress into the twentieth century, but their women weren't given the same privilege. For them, not much had changed for the last thousand years. They had been put on this earth for the sole purpose of serving their fathers and husbands, and that was the way the men wanted to keep it.

Tonight, however, other than the difference in their clothing, Robert saw little sign of this long-standing inequality between the sexes. Indeed, it was the women who took charge of the evening's events and the men

who meekly followed their directions. As he watched
a young, beautiful woman dancing in the circle of light
from the camp fires, Robert understood why earlier
this afternoon all the men had seemed so willing to
gather and chop a ton of firewood, haul gallons of
water up from the lake and help out with the cooking. If Carla, the young woman who'd started up the
dancing, was an example of the kind of entertain-
ment in store for them tonight, any man would tote
that barge and lift that bale.

The music was provided by only two violins, a
Spanish guitar and several tambourines, but the small
group produced the most provocative sounds Robert
had ever heard. As he watched Carla's voluptuous
body swaying to a pagan beat, he couldn't help but be
affected. When she lifted her arms to entice her tall,
black-haired husband Joe to join her, Robert knew he
was breathing much too fast. It was almost a relief
when the music came to an abrupt halt. Joe picked
Carla up in his arms and the twosome disappeared into
the night.

As soon as he could draw his eyes away from the
spot where they'd vanished, Robert turned to speak to
Serena, who he'd assumed was still standing beside
him. When she wasn't, he started to go in search for
her, but then the music started again, and he found out
where she'd gone. "Oh, Lord," Robert gulped as he
watched the woman he loved so much step into the
circle of firelight.

For a moment she just stood there as if waiting for
something. Robert moved closer and her eyes met his.

In that instant she began the first exotic movements of her dance.

In the moonlight her long hair gleamed like quicksilver, and the firelight added a golden glow to her fair skin. As the tempo of the music increased, Serena twirled around and around, her full skirt a flashing rainbow of color as she whirled faster and faster. As he watched, it seemed to Robert that she captured more and more of the light, as if the moon and the stars were the source of the radiant energy that made her so special.

And maybe they were, Robert thought in bemusement, remembering how he'd once thought of her as a shimmering moonbeam that had danced into his life. No man could capture a moonbeam, but he could dance beside one. Completely dazzled by Serena's ethereal beauty, helplessly caught in the sensual web of her compelling blue gaze, Robert stepped forward as if in a hypnotic trance.

There were no words to describe the wonder she felt as Serena gave herself up to the music and the man she loved. As the pulsating sounds vibrated through her, she enticed Robert with her smile, laughing with pleasure each time their eyes met. The air between them seemed charged by electricity, the current so strong that it drew them together with a force that neither could deny even if they'd wanted to. And then, he was there, his hands on her waist, claiming what had been his from the first moment they'd laid eyes on each other.

They moved as one to the music, surrendering their bodies to the passion that flowed over and between them, to the love that glowed more brightly than a dozen camp fires. They danced as if they were the only two people left in the whole universe, as if the moon and the stars in the heavens had been put there for the sole purpose of highlighting their joyful embrace. And when the music finally reached its crescendo and swiftly died away, no one questioned their early departure. The language of love was a universal one, and all those watching understood.

Robert carried Serena swiftly across the clearing to their caravan. The second they were safely inside, they tore off their clothes, impatient for that first exquisite sensation of flesh upon flesh. Together they sank upon the cot and gave into the desire that raged like a fever in their blood. Whatever doubts either of them had concerning the future were erased by the ecstasy of a mutual passion that surged ever hotter and higher, then finally culminated in a release that sent them soaring to heights they had never reached before.

A very long time later, Robert rolled over onto his side and stared lovingly down into Serena's face. "Now I know what it means to love a gypsy, and how lucky I am that a gypsy loves me."

"I'm the lucky one," Serena murmured dreamily, reaching up to touch his beloved face.

"Next year, I think we should venture down to the Smokies. I'd like to see the place where my wife and her venerable old grandmother ran their still."

Serena's brows went up at that comment. "Since when did you consider Grannie venerable?"

"How else would you describe a woman with such great foresight?" Robert inquired. "After all, she saw us together, and sure enough, here we are."

Astonished, Serena sat up in bed. "I thought you said that Grannie's vision of us was so much nonsense and only a fool would believe it."

"Then you'd better get back down here right now," Robert declared firmly.

"Huh?"

"Haven't you heard?" he murmured softly as he tugged on her hand. "We fools just love company."

Laughing, Serena allowed herself to be pulled down beside him. "I hope you don't mind that our first child will be a daughter."

"Not at all," Robert said. "As far as I'm concerned, Grannie Heidi always knows best."

Serena closed her eyes in joyful preparation for the next in what she knew would be a lifetime of Robert's kisses. Last week Claudia Tewksberry had spoken of a continuum of being, and Serena had no reason to believe that there wasn't a connection between this earthly plane and the next. As she snuggled deeper into Robert's arms, she knew that somewhere out there, a wise old gypsy woman was smiling.

* * * * *

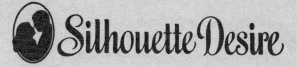

Silhouette Desire

If you liked Lass Small's **Hide and Seek** (Desire #453), you'll want to read more about the Lambert sisters in:

Blindman's Bluff (Desire #413)
Kimberly and Logan have to spend two weeks together in order to split a sizable legacy. They're both gung ho about it—until they get a look at each other!

Goldilocks and the Behr (Desire #437)
Angus Behr finds Tate's little sister Hillary in his bed. He roars about it some, but then he just can't let her go, for this she-Behr is just right!

TALES OF THE RISING MOON
A Desire trilogy by Joyce Thies

MOON OF THE RAVEN—June (#432)

Conlan Fox was part American Indian and as tough as the Montana land he rode, but it took fragile yet strong-willed Kerry Armstrong to make his dreams come true.

REACH FOR THE MOON—August (#444)

It would take a heart of stone for Steven Armstrong to evict the woman and children living on his land. But when Steven saw Samantha, eviction was the last thing on his mind!

GYPSY MOON—October (#456)

Robert Armstrong met Serena when he returned to his ancestral estate in Connecticut. Their fiery temperaments clashed from the start, but despite himself, Rob was falling under the Gypsy's spell.

In October
Silhouette Special Edition
becomes
more special than ever
as it premieres
its sophisticated new cover!

Look for six soul-satisfying novels
every month . . . from
Silhouette Special Edition

Silhouette Desire

COMING NEXT MONTH

#457 NIGHT CHILD—Ann Major
Part of the Children of Destiny trilogy. Years ago Julia Jackson had been kidnapped before young Kirk MacKay's eyes. Now an amazing turn of events offered him a second chance....

#458 CALL IT FATE—Christine Rimmer
Wealthy Reese Falconer had spurned Cassie Alden's awkward teenage advances. But when a twist of fate brought them together, he could finally take what he'd really wanted nine years before.

#459 NO HOLDS BARRED—Marley Morgan
The long-awaited prequel to *Just Joe*. When Cole Baron rescued an inebriated Jassy Creig from the honky-tonk bar, he knew there was one man she'd never be safe from—him!

#460 CHANTILLY LACE—Sally Goldenbaum
When Paul Forest investigated the mysterious pounding in his grandmother's attic, he didn't know which was more surprising—finding beautiful, dusty Rosie Hendricks...or his irresistible urge to kiss her.

#461 HIT MAN—Nancy Martin
Maggie Kincaid didn't trust Mick Spiderelli's fallen angel looks or hit man reputation, but her daughter was in danger. Soon taking care of the Kincaid women became Mick's particular specialty.

#462 DARK FIRE—Elizabeth Lowell
Cynthia McCall was thoroughly disillusioned with men *and* their motives until she met Trace Rawlings. The handsome guide was more man than she'd ever known—but could she trust her heart?

AVAILABLE NOW: